'No, Rafe, not you. You've done enough, you've literally picked up the pieces—I don't expect any more from you.'

'Maisie,' he said harshly, then paused, because the only way he knew to defuse things between them was to take her in his arms, to kiss her and cradle her to him and tell her—what?

That Mairead both attracted him and disturbed him? Because Mairead was more enigmatic than Maisie at the same time as she was— stunning. But beneath that vivacious, on-her-mettle personality, what really lay in her mind?

Lindsay Armstrong was born in South Africa, but now lives in Australia with her New Zealand-born husband and their five children. They have lived in nearly every state of Australia, and have tried their hand at some unusual—for them—occupations, such as farming and horse-training—all grist to the mill for a writer! Lindsay started writing romances when their youngest child began school and she was left feeling at a loose end. She is still doing it and loving it.

Recent titles by the same author:

FROM WAIF
TO HIS WIFE

BY
LINDSAY ARMSTRONG

MILLS & BOON
Pure reading pleasure

First published in Great Britain 2007
Harlequin Mills & Boon Limited,
Eton House, 18-24 Paradise Road, Richmond, Surrey TW9 1SR

© Lindsay Armstrong 2007

ISBN-13: 978 0 263 85363 6

Set in Times Roman 10½ on 12¾ pt
01-1007-49565

Printed and bound in Spain
by Litografía Rosés, S.A., Barcelona

FROM WAIF
TO HIS WIFE

CHAPTER ONE

MAISIE WALLIS seldom admitted defeat but on a late winter's day, not long after her twenty-second birthday, she came close to it.

She was a petite redhead with green eyes, but she presented to the world two rather different personae. Her real name was Mairead, although she'd been Maisie for as long as she could remember.

It was as the unexceptional Maisie Wallis that she taught music at a strict private school. She wasn't greatly experienced as a teacher yet, but she was passionate about music and she loved children.

It was as Mairead Wallis, with her cloud of red curls released and teased out, in stage make-up and a glitzy dress, that she pursued her second job, back-up pianist on weekends for a band that performed at upmarket receptions.

Of course, within, she was the same person. The only child of doting parents, she was a little strait-laced, she was a little unworldly, she had to acknowledge with the painful help of hindsight, although as Mairead Wallis she mightn't look it.

Then she'd lost those doting parents in a freak accident six months ago, and now she was on her own.

Well, almost, she thought as she flagged down a taxi because her car had developed a mysterious knock overnight and was in for a service; because the thought of taking a bus was nauseating and her feet were killing her, anyway.

But, as he drove her home, the taxi driver must have caught her air of despair and, as he dropped her off, he said, 'Cheer up, love! Things can't be that bad.'

She handed over the fare and was about to say that they couldn't, actually, be worse. But she stopped as she noticed a blind man walking along the pavement with a white stick and a seeing-eye dog, and she grimaced. Of course they could.

And maybe it was time to get mad, maybe the time for tears and recriminations and despair was past. She wasn't, after all, a redhead for nothing.

Moreover, Rafael Sanderson might be a high-flying, multi-millionaire with the means to keep outsiders at bay, she might have pounded the pavements in search of him today to no avail, but she refused to be treated like this.

Home was an old wooden Queenslander in Manly, a bay-side suburb of Brisbane. But it had only become home fairly recently. Her father had been in the army, so a lot of Maisie's life had been lived on the move on a variety of bases, including some overseas postings.

She'd done her music degree in Melbourne while her father had been based at Puckapunyal. Then he'd retired and her parents had fulfilled a dream; they'd moved to Queensland, the Sunshine State, they'd bought a house and a boat.

Maisie had come north as well, quite happy to move back home and be able to help her mother, who had suffered from arthritis.

The one downside, though, to being the only child of only-children parents and having moved around so much was the lack of really good friends. Not that she didn't have friends

but they were scattered far and wide and when her parents
died she hadn't been in Brisbane long enough to make the
kind of friends one could really confide in.

The house itself was comfortable although her father had
had great plans to renovate it. It also had lovely views down
to the foreshore and out over Moreton Bay to its twin guar-
dians of Moreton and North Stradbroke Islands. And it had a
garden Maisie loved pottering about in—she'd inherited her
mother's green fingers plus a cooking gene from her father.

She made herself a snack and a cup of tea. She took them
to the veranda, determined to hammer out her new resolution,
but the view captured her for a few minutes as she watched
the forest of masts in Manly Harbour, one of which belonged
to her parents' yacht, the *Amelie*, still moored in the Royal
Queensland Yacht Squadron marina.

Then she looked out over the bay and the setting sun was
laying a living carnation pink with misty violet shadows on
the steely-still waters, and it was all so lovely it brought tears
to her eyes.

She dashed them away impatiently and remembered her
resolve in the taxi. No more tears and, somehow, she would
track Rafael Sanderson down.

Starting work on her computer again recalled her extreme
surprise when she'd first started her searches, and discovered
that he was one of the richest men in Australia as CEO of
Sanderson Minerals and had inherited the Dixon pastoralist
empire.

It can't be the same one, had been her immediate reaction.
Yes, the man she was looking for had had an aura of background and substance, and the Dixon pastoralist side could
match that, but Sanderson Minerals was a giant corporation,

she discovered. Then she'd come up with a birth date that made him roughly the same age as the man she was looking for, plus some information in his curriculum vitae had made her sure he was the one…

But she couldn't help wondering why she'd never heard of him until she checked further and discovered that he was extremely reclusive. She could find business reports and articles on Sanderson Minerals and Dixon Pastoral Inc, but apart from that very potted life history, even although it had yielded gold, there was very little of a personal nature.

And images of Rafe Sanderson, she found, were as rare as hen's teeth, as her father had used to say, as well as frustratingly inconclusive. They certainly rang a bell, but there were differences that made her ponder again whether it was the same man…

Perhaps, she'd reasoned, the images she'd found were slightly misleading because they looked like press releases; they were very formal. Whereas the Rafe Sanderson she'd met had been more casual.

She'd shaken her head and decided there was just one way to find out…

It had only been by resorting to the electoral roll that she'd found a residential address. He wasn't listed in the phone book.

Sanderson Minerals did have their head office in Brisbane, but after she'd phoned, then called in person, she'd come away in no doubt whatsoever that without stating her business she had no hope of an appointment with Mr Sanderson; anyway, he was away.

She'd buzzed the address she'd gleaned from the electoral roll, a luxurious apartment block on the Brisbane River, only to receive the same disembodied message via the intercom.

That was when she'd thought to use the Dixon connection, he was a Dixon on his mother's side and the Dixons were a very old, wealthy family. One of the reasons she was so footsore today was that she'd visited several residences she'd found in the phone book in expensive suburbs like Ascot, Clayfield and Hamilton that might be the home of the very exclusive Dixon family.

One of them had, indeed, but she'd had the door shut in her face when she'd requested help in getting in touch with Rafe Sanderson.

She gritted her teeth at the memory and stiffened her spine. She would continue trawling the web until she found something that led her to him.

Fortunately the school holidays had just started, so it didn't matter if she burnt the candle at both ends. All the same, she nearly missed it. An article in an online yachting magazine that just happened to mention Rafe Sanderson's *Mary-Lue* taking line honours in an ocean race.

She blinked as the words on the screen danced before her eyes. That was all there was, although she scrolled through the article several times, noting that it was about six months old, but her mind was jumping and her fingers were suddenly shaky.

Right here under her nose all this time, she marvelled, because she knew the *Mary-Lue*. It was moored on the same finger as her parents' boat in the marina. Or, at least, she'd seen it there once and stopped to admire its sleek, green-hulled beauty. But was it still there, and was it the same *Mary-Lue?*

It was too late to do anything about it that night but the next day, after she'd picked up her car, she went down to the marina, ostensibly to check out the *Amelie*; start the motor and run the bilges.

As usual—she did it regularly—it broke her heart to be reminded of the happy days she and her parents had spent on the yacht, sailing the bay. She knew the time was approaching when she'd have to make a decision about the *Amelie*—keep it or sell it. Along with a whole lot of other decisions…

But she steeled herself and after doing her checks, she strolled down the finger in the wintry sunshine.

The *Mary-Lue* was still there in all her fifty-foot glory. Not only that, but there was also a gas bottle bearing a paper label beside it on the finger.

She glanced down to read the writing and saw that it said 'Deliver to R. Sanderson, Mary-Lue, RQ H29.'

Bingo, she thought with her heart suddenly beating heavily. RQ was the affectionate acronym of the Royal Queensland Yacht Squadron and H29 was stencilled on the pier pole indicating the berth number.

Then she had a further stroke of luck. The young lad who helped the marina manager in the school holidays stepped off the *Mary-Lue* and greeted her cheerfully.

'Hi, Maisie. Going sailing?'

'No, Travis, I've just done my usual checks and balances,' she replied. 'I thought I'd wander down the finger and see what's new.'

'Well, this gorgeous girl is going out.' He patted the *Mary-Lue's* hull. 'First light tomorrow morning, which is beaut because he hasn't had the time to take her out for months. Such a shame.' Travis, Maisie well knew, was mad about boats and sailing.

And as he hefted the gas bottle on his shoulder and climbed up to stow it on board, she called up, 'Maybe you'd like to come sailing with me one day, Travis?'

'You just name the day, Maisie,' he called back. 'See you.'

* * *

Maisie walked back to her car with a very strange sensation in the pit of her stomach.

Now that it was almost upon her—and she would do it, she knew—how was she going to feel about confronting Rafe Sanderson?

It was four o'clock the next morning when she let herself onto H finger again. She wore a navy tracksuit, deck shoes and a beanie—it was overcast, no moon or stars, and colder than she'd thought it would be. Sunrise wouldn't be for another two hours.

She made her way down the jetty finger between the boats and she sighed with relief to see the *Mary-Lue* still there, but with no sign of lights or life.

Then she almost immediately saw difficulties. What was she going to do with herself until he arrived?

There was no one about in the dark chill of a very early morning and it was tempting to climb aboard the *Mary-Lue* and make herself comfortable in the cockpit until he arrived, but that was hardly ethical.

On the other hand, how ethical was the *Mary-Lue's* owner?

She stuck out her chin and swiftly climbed aboard.

The cockpit was comfortably lined with padded seats with waterproof covers, but it was also freezing.

Perhaps you needed to think this out a little better, Maisie, she told herself, and tried, quite sure it would be locked, the door that led down to the yacht's main cabin.

It wasn't locked. She hesitated. This could definitely be putting her outside the law, but what was the worst law she was breaking—trespass? And she could always explain.

A patter of raindrops decided the matter for her. She eased open the door, slipped down the companionway and found herself in a dimly lit cabin of sumptuous comfort, from what she could see. It was also warm.

She sat down on a built-in couch. She ran through everything she planned to say to Rafe Sanderson and how she planned to say it. She heard the eutectic refrigeration click in from shore power a couple of times. She yawned.

She hadn't been able to sleep at all because of the mixture of dread and uncertainty that was building within her, but she did everything to keep herself awake bar prop her eyelids open with matchsticks. She wasn't even aware of gradually toppling over, pulling a scatter cushion beneath her cheek and falling asleep.

She was to think later that it was being used to boats and the noises they made, on top of a wakeful night, that saw her sleep like a baby through what followed.

It had never occurred to her that Rafe Sanderson would sling a bag on board, that he would loosen his lines and the electricity cable and toss them on board then climb aboard himself. That he would start the motor and, when it fired, expertly un-loop the last rope holding the boat to the jetty and reverse out of the berth without coming down to the cabin first.

In fact, she only woke when he'd steered the *Mary-Lue* out of the harbour and into the channel, and what woke her then she could never afterwards recall.

She sat up with a suddenly pounding heart and a dry mouth to see patchy sunlight coming through the portholes, and to feel the unmistakable motion of a boat underway, to hear the purr of a motor.

She closed her eyes in horror. Then she jumped up and climbed the companionway and catapulted out of the door at the head of the stairs that she'd closed so carefully to keep the cold out.

The next few minutes were chaotic. Rafe Sanderson had abandoned the wheel, put the steering on autopilot and, it appeared, had climbed up to set his mainsail.

Her unexpected arrival in the cockpit took him completely by surprise; the boom, which he'd just released, responded to the fluke breeze and hit him in the midriff and with a yell he slipped sideways, and toppled overboard.

Maisie stared in round-eyed horror this time. Then she came to life. She scrambled up and secured the boom to avoid decapitation. She hopped back down into the cockpit, studied the controls for a moment then put the motor into Neutral.

Finally she looked around wildly, spotted an orange lifesaver buoy, untied it and threw it with all her might at Rafe Sanderson's bobbing head as he swam towards the boat.

It hit him on the head—fortunately the buoy was the soft variety—but, although he grabbed it and hauled himself in, it seemed to be the final insult added to injury for him. There was no doubting it was a murderously angry, dripping man who hauled himself over the transom.

A couple of strides brought him up to her, where he took her by the shoulders and proceeded to demonstrate that he'd like to shake the life out of her.

Maybe that was what he would have done if they both hadn't frozen at the sight of a channel marker passing by on their port side, uncomfortably close.

He swore, released her and grabbed the wheel at the same time as he flicked the autopilot off.

'What the hell do you think you're doing?' he demanded furiously as he put the power on and steered the boat into the middle of the channel. 'Who the hell are you and how did you get on board?'

'I—I,' she stammered, 'I needed to talk to you, but it was freezing so I went down into the cabin to wait for you, that's all. I must have fallen asleep.'

'You mean you broke into the cabin!' he fired back at her.

'I didn't! It wasn't locked, so—'

'Oh, yes, it was!'

'No, it wasn't,' she insisted. 'Do I look like the kind of girl who goes around breaking locks?'

'You look like,' he paused and scanned her, 'heaven knows what! How on earth could I tell…' He stopped impatiently then frowned. 'Maybe not. You look about sixteen but I suppose you could have taken to a life of crime early!'

But Maisie was now looking at him in something like horror. 'Who—who are you?' she stammered.

'What's that got to do with anything?' he rasped. 'How did you get in?'

'Well,' she swallowed convulsively, as her mind did cartwheels, 'um—the door wasn't locked. Maybe you had a delivery and someone from the marina office brought it on board and forgot to lock the door behind them?'

She stopped and flinched inwardly as she thought belatedly of Travis, the last person she wanted to blame, especially as she might have distracted him herself.

'I…' He paused. 'I did have a catering package delivered and a new gas bottle,' he said almost to himself, then shrugged. 'That still gives you no right to be on my boat. Here, take the bloody wheel,' he added roughly. 'You may have all but drowned me, you may have tried to knock me out, but you're not going to finish me off with pneumonia. Red to starboard, green to port,' he said, indicating the channel markers.

'I kn-know that,' Maisie said a little shakily as she stepped up to the wheel, 'but shouldn't we be turning back?'

'Like f... Like hell we should,' he amended, still blazingly angry as he started to pull off his sodden sweater.

'You don't have to not swear on my account, if it makes you feel better,' she said nervously as she took over the steering. 'I've probably heard it all before.'

'I doubt it. But just in case you haven't seen it all before you might like to keep your eyes ahead.'

Of course, she turned to look a question at him automatically, only to see that he'd stripped and was pulling a towel out of his bag.

'Oh,' she said, and felt her cheeks start to burn as she switched her gaze to dead straight ahead. For, whoever this was, he was superb. Streamlined, finely muscled with compact hips, a washboard stomach, long legs—he'd be an artist's dream model, not to mention the answer to most girls' prayers.

Nor did it escape her attention that his naked body had caused a fluttery sensation in the pit of her stomach, which caused her serious consternation and disbelief...

'Oh?' he echoed.

'I didn't realise that's what you meant, that's all. Sorry.'

He growled something unintelligible and presently came back into sight, dressed in dry clothes, to take the wheel from her.

'Now, ma'am, miss, boat burglar or whatever you are, we need some hot coffee.'

Maisie hesitated. 'I really do think we should turn around—'

'Then you shouldn't have sneaked aboard,' he said drily, 'because I planned to sail to Horseshoe Bay on Peel Island this morning, I've invited two couples from other boats aboard for lunch and that is still my intention. Off you go!'

Maisie went. She had no idea what else she could do at that moment.

Under normal circumstances, unless your mind was going round in circles, it would have been a pleasure to make coffee aboard the *Mary-Lue*.

The sumptuousness of the main cabin was revealed in all its glory in daylight. The mellow rich gleam of New Guinea rosewood was polished to perfection. The navy cut-velvet upholstery was lifted with turquoise scatter cushions and turquoise carpeting, and a brass lamp with a gold foil shade stood on the bar.

There was a built-in chart table and a duplicate set of controls, a radar, GPS and plotter, plus a variety of marine radios. You could go anywhere on the *Mary-Lue*, she thought.

The galley was spotless and had every mod con including an ice-maker. No plastic glasses and mugs—instead she found crystal glasses and a set of fine china coffee mugs that echoed the décor in their pattern of navy, turquoise and gold.

She could only find instant coffee, however, but when she opened the fridge for milk it was to see it was stocked with pâtés and exotic cheeses, smoked salmon and oysters, a lobster salad, strawberries, six bottles of champagne and much more. She assembled the coffee on a tray and bore it carefully up the stairs.

The man at the wheel bent down to take it from her, and she emerged into the cockpit to see he'd taken the waterproof covers off the seats.

His short, thick hair had also started to dry, so she could see it was dark blond; ditto, she thought. Height? About six feet four—ditto, she thought again—and grey eyes, but it was definitely not the same man, with a very different aura.

She closed her eyes in confusion then opened them to notice the sky hadn't cleared completely, so there was patchy sunlight, and it was still cool. What breeze there was was errant so that the surface of the water was glassy and reflecting the sky, then lightly ruffled.

Peel Island, coming up on their port bow, was low and green compared to the bulk of North Stradebroke behind it. There was not much activity on this part of Moreton Bay on this chilly Saturday morning.

'Sit down,' he ordered, 'and start talking.'

Maisie did everything she knew to compose herself in what was not only a mystifying but also a dreadfully embarrassing situation.

She took some deep breaths then remembered she was still wearing her beanie. She took it off and ran her fingers through her hair and the breeze lifted her curls, causing her companion to narrow his eyes as he studied her.

Finally, she wrapped her hands around her mug. 'W-would you please tell me who you are first? I do—really—need to know.'

'Rafe Sanderson,' he said curtly. 'More to the point, who are you?'

'No, you're not.' The words slipped out before she could help herself but she meant them.

He looked at her ironically. 'I can assure you I am.'

'But I happen to know you're not!'

'Now look here—how?' He changed tack slightly. 'I can guarantee we don't know each other from a—the proverbial bar of soap.'

'That's just it,' she cried and lost all caution to the wind.

'I—I had an affair with Rafe Sanderson, if you could call it that. I'm pregnant with his baby, but it would appear he's—he doesn't want anything more to do with me.'

He was stunned into silence for a good minute. Then he put the motor into Neutral, then Reverse, and as the boat stopped moving he let out the anchor chain with a touch of a button on the console.

And Maisie continued a little desperately, 'At first I thought you were him, and now I see you're not, but it's the same name so I—I'm terribly confused.'

'Some girls are easy to confuse,' he said then with a hard little glint in his grey eyes. 'Go on.'

'You don't believe me,' Maisie said and gestured. 'To be honest, neither do I. Not that it didn't happen but I don't believe I could have let it—'

'Were you coerced?' he asked abruptly.

'No.' And suddenly the fact that she'd had no one to confide in claimed her and it all spilt out. 'I was lonely and bereft. I'd lost my parents—we were very close—a couple of months beforehand. Then one day I was doing my Mairead Wallis act—'

'What the hell is that?'

She told him about her name and the band. 'And when we'd finished playing—it was an afternoon wedding—this man came up and introduced himself as Rafael Sanderson and asked if he could buy me a drink. I said no, thanks, but a cup of coffee would be nice. It all started there.'

'Did you climb into bed with him that night?'

'No,' she said coldly and felt some of her redheadedness seep into her veins.

Then she paused to take charge of her emotions, which also included being unable to deny that she'd been incredibly naïve.

'But I really enjoyed his company, he was charming, funny

and—gorgeous. And life just didn't seem to be so bleak any more.' She stopped and sighed. 'So we had a few dates…for some reason I really dressed up for him, then he told me he'd fallen in love with me on sight and he wanted to marry me.'

She closed her eyes. 'I *believed* him. So, then, it did happen. I'll never know if it was the wine we had—I don't usually drink—but,' she looked down at her hands, 'I also believed him when he said he'd take charge of things.'

'Contraception?'

She nodded.

'He didn't,' he said flatly, 'and if all this is to be believed, he skedaddled. So it only happened once? Although I presume it rang bells and blew trumpets for you?'

'It didn't, actually.' She looked self-conscious. 'I mean, it was fine, but…' She trailed off, looking embarrassed.

'The earth didn't move for you?' he suggested.

'Well, no, but I was a virgin and I thought it was just going to take time. And he was—well, he was nice about it and reassuring and I felt wanted, I felt loved…' She trailed off and gestured.

Bastard, Rafe caught himself thinking. If any of this is to be believed. 'So—only once?' he queried sceptically.

She nodded again, but if he'd known her better he would have intercepted the little glint in her green eyes, and interpreted it correctly.

'And that's when you started to search for Rafael Sanderson?'

'That's when it occurred to me I had no means of getting in touch with him; he'd always been the one to make contact. That's when I started to worry, not only on my account. I wondered if he'd had an accident—I was terribly concerned and confused, so—' she shrugged '—but the only Rafael Sanderson, in Australia anyway, that I came up with turned out to be the CEO of Sanderson Minerals and heir to the Dixon fortune! Then I found out I was pregnant.'

He scanned her figure. 'You don't look it. Listen, this is all very touching—'

But Maisie slammed her fists on the table and shot up from her seat.

'Don't think,' she spat at him, 'I haven't reflected on my stupidity, at great and bitter length, in fact. Don't think that the real irony is I was the last girl I thought this could happen to, and it's shocked me to my boots to discover I was as vulnerable as many other girls who find themselves in this position. But don't think I intend to take it lying down, either.'

She paused and flinched at her choice of words as he raised an eyebrow drily, then she soldiered on. 'So you may look at me as cynically as you like, whoever you are, but I intend to find this man and give him a piece of my mind if nothing else!'

'Sit down, Mairead—'

'Maisie,' she shot back.

'I thought you said—'

'I did, but I'm mostly called Maisie and, if you must know, I've become a bit allergic to Mairead because I suspect she led Rafe into believing I'm more—worldly than I am. Make that *was*!'

'He wasn't Rafe, I am,' he pointed out with a sudden look of amusement. 'I'm afraid you've got your men well and truly mixed up and I'm not sure it's quite unintentionally, Mair—pardon me, *Maisie,* so—'

'Well, I'm afraid to say I can't stand your superior, mocking company a moment longer,' she interrupted vigorously, with unconscious hauteur stamped into every line of her body.

And she climbed onto the gunnel and dived neatly overboard.

CHAPTER TWO

IT WASN'T quite as unplanned or as insane as it looked.

In the moments before she did it, it flashed through her mind that the tide was going out, it wasn't any great swim to the shallows and reefs around Peel, which were starting to be exposed anyway, and she was a good swimmer.

And once she got to the island she could walk to Lazaret's Gutter, where she could see boats anchored, and get some help.

Two things worked against her. The shock of the cold water and the fact that the tide was running more swiftly than she'd anticipated.

Nor did she anticipate the speed with which Rafe Sanderson would get the *Mary-Lue's* inflatable dinghy down into the water off its davits.

As she struggled against the tide, though, it was with a sense of gratitude that she saw the dinghy streaking towards her.

But once again it was a murderously angry man who man-handled her into the dinghy then onto the *Mary-Lue*.

'Don't you ever do that again, you idiot!' he stormed at her, gripping the lapels of her tracksuit top in his fists as they stood in the cockpit, lifting her on to her tiptoes.

It was only natural that some of Maisie's fire would be

quenched. She was dripping, she was freezing, she was feeling slightly foolish.

But enough of a spark remained, fanned by her feeling of extreme ill-use, for her to retort, albeit through chattering teeth, 'I'd have m-made it if it hadn't b-been for the tide.' She paused then yelled at the top of her voice, 'And you have done nothing but insult me!'

Furious grey eyes looked into furious green ones, then Rafe Sanderson relaxed suddenly, and drawled, 'So. A real firebrand? My apologies, Maisie.' He released her lapels and she sank back onto her heels. 'Anyway, perhaps this will make amends.'

He pulled her into his arms.

How it should affect her so drastically considering she was half drowned, not to mention furious with him, Maisie had no idea. But she had the strangest feeling that anything was possible between her and Rafe Sanderson at that moment.

It was as if such a level of tension in her had to expose her to the other side of the coin, or as if you could only be that angry with a man over how he viewed you because you wanted to be viewed differently...

But these jumbled thoughts were no protection against the way she felt as his arms closed round her.

Her confusion, tension and anger seemed to evaporate slowly. She found herself feeling safe and not so much like a piece of flotsam tossed without warning on the stormy seas of life. Not to mention the swift-running, freezing water she'd cast herself into.

Then he bent his head to kiss her and his lips were warm and dry and new sensations stirred in her. Sensations that shocked her to her core. How could she enjoy a man's hands on her, his mouth on hers, how could she feel all stirred up in that particularly delicious way when it had led her into such a terrible trap only months ago?

He kissed her briefly, not even parting her lips, then lifted his head and stared into her green eyes, so wide and so shocked but at variance with the unresisting way she stood in the circle of his arms.

And something she couldn't read flickered in his expression before he let her go. Then he immediately started to undress her.

Maisie came back to earth with a thud.

'No,' she gasped, 'no!' And attempted to stop him.

'Listen,' he commanded, 'the only reason I'm doing this is because there's no point in you dripping all over the saloon carpet—I have no designs on you!'

'But you've just k-kissed me,' she objected.

'That was something else.'

'How could it be? I mean—I mean, how do I know I won't end up discarded and pregnant again?'

He paused and looked into her eyes, very green but supremely confused and wary, and a faint smile touched his lips. 'I don't think you can be pregnant twice at the same time.'

She bit her lip in frustration. 'You know what I mean.'

He shrugged. 'It was to make up for insulting you and being all superior and cynical. It was a salute for being told to go to hell in a rather foolhardy, but nevertheless decisive manner I couldn't help admiring. That's all.'

Maisie stared at him, uncharacteristically speechless, and he took the opportunity to strip off her top and push her trousers down then he sat her down so he could take off her shoes.

'Besides which,' he added, 'I have seen it all before.'

'But—but…'

He scanned her delicate figure beneath an emerald-green

bra patterned with pink frangipanis and matching bikini briefs, and raised an eyebrow. 'Very fetching, Maisie, but believe me, you're not my type so you're quite safe. Up you get!'

He pulled her to her feet as a wave of telltale colour mounted in her cheeks, and picked her up to carry her downstairs.

'Right, into the shower, we've got plenty of hot water, so don't stint until you feel warm right through,' he ordered and set her on her feet as he opened the bathroom door.

'But I've got no clothes!'

'I'll find you some. Just do as you're told.'

The hot water was wonderful but she finally stepped out and wrapped her slim body in a towel and wrapped another, smaller one round her head. Then she realised that the boat was underway again and wondered in which direction he was going—Manly or Peel?

There was a rap on the door.

'Yes?' she called.

'Go through the other door,' Rafe Sanderson instructed. 'It leads into the aft berth and you'll find some clothes on the bed. Don't take too long—once I've got the anchor down I'll be making a warm drink for you.'

'Yes, sir; no, sir; three bags full,' Maisie murmured beneath her breath, but she did as she was told.

The aft berth had a walk-around double bed with a toffee and peppermint quilted silk coverlet. Her feet sank into deep toffee-coloured carpet, and the fittings were again New Guinea rosewood with brass handles.

She dropped the towel and looked down at herself. She was about three and a half months pregnant but if anything she'd lost a bit of weight. She put that down to stress and the fact that she'd gone through a period of morning sickness—only at night, thankfully, so it hadn't affected her job—but it had quite put her off food.

Fortunately, that phase had mostly gone quite recently, although she still got the odd twinge. It was also fortunate it had passed because feeling physically dreadful a lot of the time, on top of feeling mentally traumatised, had seen her dither around unable to do anything or make any decisions.

But the only difference so far she could see in her body, apart from the bit of weight she'd lost, was her breasts. Her nipples were darker and more sensitive.

She turned her attention to the pile of clothes on the bed. They were a shade too big for her but she couldn't quibble about their quality.

She pulled on coffee silk and lace knickers that looked to be brand-new. There was a matching bra but it was too big for her, so she chose a cream singlet with a prim satin bow. Then she put on a pair of green track pants and finally a gloriously snug cream-coloured cable-knit sweater.

It definitely wasn't new, although it was perfectly clean, but a subtle perfume lingered on the wool.

Whose clothes were these she wondered.

There were no shoes but a pair of socks.

Finally, she looked at herself in the fitted dressing-table mirror. Her irrepressible hair was already starting to curl riotously but since she had nothing to tie it back with she could only comb her fingers through it. But it was the expression in her eyes that really startled her.

She looked somewhat shell-shocked, she decided. But who wouldn't after diving overboard and having to be rescued? Or was it something to do with being kissed then being dismissed into a "not my type" category?

Of course I'm not his type, she thought immediately. Apart

from anything else I'm pregnant by another man. But how did he make me feel so safe and…?

He did save me, she reminded herself as her cheeks started to warm.

Then she heard the different pitch of the motor, indicating slower revs then neutral, and the anchor chain rattled out. She looked out of the porthole to recognise the curved white beach of Horseshoe Bay on Peel Island, and bit her lip.

A few minutes later, as she was trying to work out how to deal with this development, he called out that coffee was ready.

'How do you feel?' he enquired as they sat opposite each other in the dining section.

This time there was proper, steaming coffee poured from a stainless-steel pot, and there was a dash of brandy in it.

'I… Fine,' she answered. 'A lot warmer. Uh—thanks for the clothes.'

'They belong to my sister, Sonia, who comes sailing with me from time to time—in case you're wondering,' he said with a dry little look.

'I…' Maisie glanced away awkwardly then decided not to pursue the matter.

'Hmm… Well, you've got a bit of colour back in your cheeks. Are you really pregnant?' he said then.

She blinked. 'Why?'

'Because if you are you should curb your apparently natural instincts towards outrageous deeds—like diving off boats and battling the tide,' he added laconically.

Maisie's hands flew protectively to her stomach. 'I didn't stop to think,' she breathed. 'But the doctor did tell me there was no need to cosset myself.'

He raised an eyebrow. 'His version of cosset could differ from yours. However, that seems to answer both my questions.'

'Both?'

'Yes. Not only are you pregnant, but you also don't like the thought of losing the baby.' His eyes searched hers.

'No, I don't.' Maisie sipped her coffee and tried to find the words to explain.

Because out of the blue, amidst the shock and growing horror of finding herself pregnant and abandoned, the thought had dropped into her mind that she would not be alone in the world now.

She'd examined it carefully from all angles, but none of the obstacles, and her life was going to be strewn with them because of this baby, could douse that thought and it had grown stronger...

'I—I—would have *someone*, you see,' she said at last.

He said nothing but she felt as if that steady grey gaze was probing right through to her soul. Then, 'How old are you?'

'Twenty-two.'

He grimaced. 'So are you hoping for some kind of a settlement from this—this man?'

'No.' She tilted her chin. 'If he doesn't want anything more to do with me, I certainly don't want his charity. But if he has no good reason other than he's a—a cad and a bounder,' sudden tears shone in her eyes, 'who goes around preying on girls, I want to be able to tell him he's a—he's a—'

'An utter bastard?' he supplied.

She nodded then moved her hands expressively. 'Not only that. I need, even if he doesn't want anything to do with us, him to agree to having his name on the baby's birth certificate. I feel I owe the baby nothing less—to at least know who its father is—wouldn't you?'

He didn't comment on that directly. He said instead, 'You've obviously given it a lot of thought.'

'I've had several increasingly miserable months to think of nothing else.' She wiped her eyes impatiently at the same time as she added an admonition to herself in an undertone, 'No more tears, Maisie!'

Then she was struck by another thought. 'But now I haven't even got a name—unless there is another man with the same name out there!'

Rafe Sanderson watched her and thought his own thoughts. Was she a superb actress he wondered.

Had she hit on an original twist for an old and sorry story? Such as finding herself pregnant and abandoned and deciding to make the best of it? Such as picking his name at random, well, from amongst the suitably well heeled, and concocting a likely tale along the lines of—*he said he was you and I really believed him*.

His eyes narrowed as he followed the thought. It would have taken a bit of planning. First of all, she'd have had to come up with an uncommon name—she'd probably have had to check that out in Queensland at least—and his did fit the bill. But if so, and the rest of it was a pack of lies, what had she been hoping for?

That he'd be so touched by her plight and her pluck, he'd hand over some cash to help her out?

He smiled a grim, austere little smile then looked across at her to find her studying him intently.

'You're not believing me again,' she said huskily.

'Maisie,' he gestured, 'whatever, and I'm sorry for anyone in this position, but it's not my affair.'

'Did you ever live at a place called Karoo Downs?' she queried. 'A sheep station out west somewhere?'

He frowned. 'How did you know that?'

'As a matter of fact, it's common knowledge if you'd like to look it up on the internet. Apparently there was a South African connection in the Dixon family in the early days and Karoo comes from the Great Karoo in South Africa, also sheep country.'

'You've done your research well,' he said flatly.

'Oh, I knew about Karoo Downs before I started searching,' she said. 'R...he told me about it. He also told me about his two favourite dogs, Graaff and Reinet.'

Rafe Sanderson suddenly drummed his fingers on the table.

'I asked about the names,' Maisie continued. 'He said Graaff-Reinet is the main town in the Karoo and these two dogs were ridgebacks, a South African breed originally, and that's why he chose the names.'

This time Rafe Sanderson swore. 'Who the bloody hell have you been talking to, Maisie?'

'No one. No one else. Oh, a Dixon who shut the door in my face, only two days ago as it happens.'

'You must have been. Family, staff.' He narrowed his eyes on her. 'Listen, Maisie, I want the truth and now,' he said through his teeth.

'The truth?' She stared at him with her lips parted and her eyes widening. 'There must be some man out there going around impersonating you...'

He banged his fist on the table and made the coffee mugs jump. 'Now I've heard it all.'

'But for a few minutes I thought you were him,' she protested. 'I mean, now I'm quite sure you're not and if you hadn't been dripping wet and so angry I might have realised sooner...' She stopped bewilderedly. 'But I did think so at first.'

He opened his mouth to retort but the VHF radio above the charting desk came alive and intervened. '*Mary-Lue,*

Mary-Lue—Lotus Lady, six seven,' a deep, disembodied voice said.

Rafe shut his mouth with a click then got up to answer the call. '*Lotus Lady—Mary-Lue*, six nine.' And he changed channels.

'Rafe—Dan here; we'll be over in about twenty minutes. Melissa wants to know if there's anything you need—and we'll pick up Eddie and Martha on the way.'

Rafe Sanderson hesitated and glanced darkly at Maisie. Then he depressed his PTT button and said into the mike, 'Don't need anything, thanks, mate. See you soon.' He hung up the mike and came back to the table.

Maisie swallowed and suddenly looked desperately tired and uneasy. 'How are you going to explain me to your friends?'

He took in her wan complexion. 'I'm not. Are you sure you're feeling all right?'

'I'm fine but tired, that's all. I—I didn't sleep last night and I probably only had an hour here before you came on board. I also—sometimes I just feel like a cat who needs to curl up and go to sleep.'

'Then go to bed, kid,' he said, not unkindly. 'Use the aft berth. With a bit of luck no one will even know you're here. We can get down to brass tacks again,' he looked impatient for a moment, 'later.'

'Oh, thank you,' Maisie said with real gratitude.

'Just one thing.'

She looked a query at him.

'I need you to promise me you won't try to drown yourself again, you won't try to drown *me* or do anything else outrageous.'

Maisie had to laugh. 'I promise,' she said, 'unless, that is, your behaviour is outrageous, Mr Sanderson.'

He studied her with a faint frown in his eyes, as if he didn't quite know what to make of her. Then he shrugged and got up.

Maisie fell asleep with no difficulty.

She tried not to. She told herself there was too much to think about, too much to attempt to clarify, not least her re-action to a man she'd only just met, but nothing could keep at bay the tide of weariness that overcame her.

She didn't hear the lunch party come aboard, she didn't hear anything until she woke a couple of hours later.

She stretched, yawned and looked around with no idea where she was until the toffee and peppermint décor struck a chord.

She sat up abruptly in time to hear a female voice above deck, saying,

'Why, Rafe, you've got a girl in your cabin!'

Maisie froze, and realised that it must have been the opening, or more likely the closing, of the cabin door that had woken her.

'Melissa,' Rafe's voice sounding irritable, 'hasn't anyone told you to wait for an invitation before you nose about?'

A tinkle of laughter, then, 'Darling, life's too short to wait for invitations. And, unless I'm very much mistaken, she's a redhead.'

Maisie waited with bated breath.

'She's also a stowaway I'd never laid eyes on until she made her presence known and nearly drowned me,' Rafe replied coolly. 'What's more she's going back from whence she came, wherever the hell that is, pronto, which is why I'm about to throw you lot off. I need to get underway.'

'Well, darling,' Melissa said, 'however you want to call it is fine by us. And thanks for a lovely lunch. We might toddle off and spend the night at Blakesley's anchorage. Oh. Will we see you at Tricia's party on Wednesday?'

Rafe Sanderson replied in the negative.

Maisie waited, as she heard the sound of an outboard motor revving then receding, before she got up and made her way to the main saloon, not at all sure of her reception in light of Rafe's blunt and truthful explanation of her presence, and how he planned to handle her dismissal.

He surprised her. He came down the steps at the same time, raised an eyebrow at her and asked her if she was hungry.

Maisie closed her eyes. 'I—I'm starving! No breakfast, no lunch.'

'That's what I thought, so I kept you some food.' He withdrew some foil-wrapped plates from the fridge and set them on the table.

A minor feast greeted her eyes as he unwrapped the foil. Smoked salmon and melon; cold lobster in a salad studded with black olives and feta cheese, accompanied by a crispy chicken leg and a slice of quiche which he removed and warmed in the microwave. He also warmed two rolls.

'Thank you so much,' she murmured as she gazed hungrily at his offerings. She hesitated. 'I rather thought you were going to make me walk the plank.'

'You heard?'

'I heard. She must have woken me when she closed the door.'

'She can be the most infuriating woman, but Dan is a good friend,' he said. 'As for making you walk the plank, I'm feeding you and making you a cup of tea instead because cruelty to pregnant ladies is not amongst my vices. However,' he paused to fill the kettle, 'as soon as you've eaten, we are going straight back to Manly.'

Maisie ate the salmon and melon. 'Where you intend to wash your hands of me?'

He looked at her expressionlessly over his shoulder then lit the gas and put the kettle on the hob. 'As a matter of fact, I intend to leave no stone unturned until I get to the bottom of this.'

Maisie demolished the lobster and the quiche then she picked up the chicken leg and sank her teeth into it. When she finished, she wiped her fingers fastidiously on the paper napkin he'd supplied.

'You were hungry,' he commented.

She smiled ruefully. 'For weeks I was as sick as a dog and could hardly look food in the face; now I'm ravenous most of the time.' She hesitated. 'Does that mean you believe me?'

He poured two cups of tea and came to sit down. 'No, but neither do I disbelieve you. You could say I'm reserving judgement, but if there is some bastard going around out there impersonating me, I intend to nail him.'

Maisie shivered involuntarily.

He noted it and pressed home his advantage. 'But if there isn't, this is the time to come clean, Maisie Wallis,' he added quietly, but in a way that left her in no doubt he meant it.

'That's exactly how it happened.' She lifted her shoulders. 'Why would I make up such a story?'

'Do you really need me to answer that?'

'Yes, I do!' Her green eyes were indignant.

'OK, then, women have been throwing themselves in my path for years,' he said deliberately. 'Don't think I enjoy it or flatter myself that my money isn't the draw, I don't. And this could be an original way of doing it.

'No,' he added as Maisie drew a deep breath, 'the time for furious displays of anger is past, straight-talking is what we need now, Maisie. For example, when you said the only Rafael

Sanderson you could come up with was me, does that mean the name meant nothing to you when this man introduced himself as me?'

'No—yes! I'd never heard of you.'

'So why would anyone masquerade as me to a girl it meant nothing to?'

Maisie's eyes widened. 'I have no idea,' she whispered.

'But you assumed there was a bit of substance in his background all the same?'

'I honestly didn't give it much thought but I suppose so. He was well-spoken, he'd travelled, he was,' she grimaced, 'a lot more sophisticated than anyone else I'd ever dated.'

He smiled a lethal little smile. 'Well, that's the kind of thing I'll be digging into, as well as your background and so on. Do you really want me to go on with it?'

For a moment, Maisie was in two minds as it struck her that this Rafael Sanderson had an aura his impersonator—and it had to be that—had lacked.

Yes, there were physical similarities, colouring, height and so on.

This Rafe had changed again, after rescuing her and kissing her, during which a fair bit of her drenched condition had transferred itself to him, into jeans and a grey, fine-wool round-necked sweater.

With his thick, ruffled dark-blond hair, those unusual eyes, his lean, strong lines beneath his jeans and sweater, and with his beautiful hands, she noticed suddenly, he was just as attractive.

Similar build—glorious physiques in other words, similar good looks, but—two very different characters, she reflected.

The first Rafe had been charming, he'd been easy-going, he'd really made her laugh at the same time as he'd made her feel desirable and able to view the world a little less darkly in his company.

Yet, despite allusions to a wealthy background, she would never have taken him for the CEO of a minerals corporation, whereas the man sitting opposite her struck her as exactly that.

He definitely had the aura of a clever, powerful businessman who knew what he wanted and got it. It was there in the way he spoke, in his gestures and the way he handled people. It had been there in the few images she'd brought up on her computer that had puzzled her and made her wonder if they were one and the same man.

In other words, beneath those good looks, and wonderfully honed, tall body, there was a lot more substance to this man, there was even a faintly dangerous edge to him that made you stop and think twice about tangling with him.

But she was telling the truth, she reminded herself, so what did she have to lose?

'You may do your darnedest, Mr Sanderson,' she told him quietly. 'I have nothing to hide.'

'I see.' He said it quite neutrally, but his gaze was extremely penetrating and acute.

So penetrating, Maisie found herself thinking some bizarre thoughts.

How was he seeing her?

Simply as a troublesome thorn in his side? A girl who'd got herself into trouble and was therefore beyond the pale?

Or, had any of the deliciously feminine sensations he'd aroused in her got through to him? Something had prompted him to kiss her, after all, so he'd been the one to make the first move, but…

'Good,' he said, breaking into her thoughts. 'Well, now that we've got that settled, let's make a move.' He got up and picked up her plate.

'Oh, I'll do that—unless you need me up top?'

'Thanks, but I can manage.' He turned away and ascended the steps to the deck two at a time.

Maisie watched him go and she drew a sudden, startled little breath to discover that it was far from settled for her.

His athleticism stripped away his sweater and jeans in her mind and presented her with an image of him unclothed, and her imagination ran riot.

She pictured herself on the aft berth with him laughing down at her with tender, wicked amusement as if at an intimate joke only they could share.

Her thoughts roamed on and she realised that if that amusement changed to Rafe Sanderson looking at her with heavy-lidded desire, it would send her to the moon…

Even just the thought of it, and the images that accompanied it, raised her pulses to fever pitch and left her awash with sensation all through her body.

Maisie, Maisie, she thought in some desperation, don't let this happen to you! Think of your fatherless baby if nothing else.

CHAPTER THREE

THEY didn't make it to Manly—they didn't manage to leave Horseshoe Bay.

Maisie started to clear up her late lunch, waiting expectantly to hear the yacht's motor fire, which it did, only to be cut off after a few minutes and without them moving.

She glanced expectantly at Rafe as he came downstairs, to see him looking annoyed.

'Trouble?' she hazarded.

'Yep, the motor's overheating.' He started to roll up a section of carpet in the saloon and she realised he was going into the engine room through the floorboards. 'I haven't been out on her for ages, and that's always a bad thing to do to boats.'

'I know. A problem with the cooling system?' she hazarded.

'Most likely. You're a mine of unexpected information, Maisie. How come you know so much about boats?'

She told him.

'So that's how you got onto the berth, I wondered.' He heaved up a section of floorboard. 'Could you put the engine-room light on from that switchboard?' He pointed. 'Could you also bring me the torch that's in the locker under those stairs?' He pointed again.

'Aye, aye, skipper!' She did it all, then sat down on the carpet to watch as he worked in the confined space.

After a time, she said as she heard a muffled oath, 'You've found it?'

'Yes. A broken fan belt. Listen, Maisie,' he half rose out of the depths of the engine room, rubbing his hands on a piece of waste cotton, 'this is going to take a bit of time to fix but I've got a spare. And we do have to fix it before we can move because what little wind there was has died right down, so there's no chance of sailing.'

'And fan belts can be the devil to fit,' she said ruefully. 'Just getting to them in that confined space can be a nightmare.'

'You're not wrong. So, we'll either be late or we might not make it at all.'

'Oh.'

He glanced at her. 'On the other hand, you would be quite safe with me here overnight if that's the way it pans out. If by any chance I can't fit it, I can get help out of Manly tomorrow morning.' He consulted his watch. 'It's probably too late to call anyone out now.'

Maisie looked at her own watch. It was close to five o'clock. 'All right,' she said cautiously, although it crossed her mind that no one in their right minds, no one who knew anything about boats anyway, would put themselves through a broken fan-belt situation for an ulterior motive.

'OK,' he heaved himself out of the engine room. 'I need tools and I need some old clothes.'

'I may be able to help. I often helped my father—handing him tools and so on, and sometimes, because my hands were a lot smaller than his, I could get into really tricky spots he couldn't.'

'Good on you, Ms Wallis,' he murmured and went down to the forward cabin. He came back shortly wearing an old khaki shirt and clean but stained jeans and carrying a tool bag. And he lowered himself once again into the bowels of the boat.

The job took them several hours.

Maisie handed him tools, directed the torch light and once did manage to get her hand into a tricky spot to attach a socket spanner where he couldn't reach.

Finally he asked her to start the motor and watch the temperature gauge like a hawk.

'It's normal,' she called down the companionway after running the motor for about ten minutes.

'Good. Switch off,' he called back and stiffly and wearily climbed out. He stretched. 'What I need is a drink. But thank you, Maisie,' he added as she came down. 'You make a pretty good mechanic's mate!'

'I'd say you make a pretty good mechanic,' she returned. 'Are you one?'

'No, not by trade, but I've always enjoyed tinkering around with motors. Look, I don't know about you, but I'd like a shower, a beer, something to eat then a good sleep.' He raised an eyebrow at her. 'You're welcome to lock yourself into the forward cabin if you wish,' he added. 'I would offer you the aft berth but it doesn't lock.'

Maisie considered that she'd only had about three hours' sleep in the last twenty-four hours, and suddenly had to stifle a huge yawn. 'All right,' she conceded. 'I'm just about out on my feet anyway but you go and have your shower—I'll put together a snack.'

His lips twisted. 'Yes, ma'am.'

But as Maisie heard the fresh-water pump click on, she stopped in her tracks as a mental picture of Rafe Sanderson in the shower hit her.

She could understand how stiff and cramped he must feel after a couple of hours of working in such a confined space. She could see him stretching luxuriously beneath the shower jet, she could picture the muscles of his broad shoulders flexing and the water streaming down his long body—and she could feel her own pulses starting to race.

Then, to her horror, in her mind's eye she took her place beside him in the shower, pale and slight beside his bulk but with her breasts ripening as he lifted his hands and cupped them. As he smoothed his hands down her waist and cradled her hips and as she raised her hands and turned off the water, and offered him her mouth, flattening her body against his as she did so.

She closed her eyes and gritted her teeth to make the images go away, but nothing, for a few moments, could still the tremors of desire that ran through her...

This is getting out of hand, she thought as she made herself get to work in the galley then had to stop and take several deep breaths.

She broke off her thoughts and bit her lip, and as the water pump clicked off she forced herself to concentrate on the task at hand, not to mention banishing any more wild and wanton fantasies.

The snack she produced was along the same lines as the lunch he'd produced for her. And she poured a beer into a long glass for him, while she had an orange juice.

They ate companionably in the saloon. It was peaceful with the soft lap of water against the hull as they ate by lamplight and at one stage she asked him exactly what he did.

'I'm a geologist and a mining engineer by profession and I know a bit about sheep.'

She looked at him consideringly. He'd changed again into jeans and a warm tartan shirt. His hair was still damp and bore comb marks. 'I don't suppose you do much of either these days.'

He rubbed his jaw. 'You suppose right. Since my father died, I seem to spend most of my time travelling.'

'Do you enjoy that?'

He laid his head back against the settee and shrugged. 'It comes with the territory. It would not,' he paused, and wondered why it had occurred to him, 'go well with a settled family life at this stage.'

'How so?' she enquired. 'I mean, you're not getting any younger—' She broke off and bit her lip.

He laughed outright. 'Out of the mouths of babes? I may look ancient to you, Maisie, but I'm only thirty-four.'

'I didn't mean that,' she assured him with a curious little spark of irony in her eyes as she thought—ancient? No, quite perfect, actually… 'I—um,' she said hastily, 'meant, well, it wouldn't be a bad time to settle down, though, would it? And perhaps you need to—uh—learn to delegate a bit?'

He gazed at her, his grey eyes wry. Then, 'No, in the normal course of events it wouldn't be a bad idea to settle down and start a family. But my father embarked on a serious expansion programme for Sanderson Minerals a few months before he died, and it's going to take me a couple of years at least to see it through. How about you?'

'Me?'

'What plans did you have before this cataclysmic event overtook you?'

She shrugged. 'The usual, I suppose. To be honest, although I probably was a bit old still to be living with my parents, I enjoyed it, I enjoy my job and,' she sighed, 'things were sailing along for me. I really love travelling, I spent a month backpacking in Mexico last year and…' She gestured.

'Tell me.'

'Well, I started a travel fund for later this year, but I'll obviously have to have a rethink there.'

'No particular grand plan?'

'Yes, one. I would like to get my master's degree in music. There's no age limit on that, luckily, so I might still achieve it.'

'Are you planning to cope on a single-mother's allowance?' he queried.

Maisie grimaced. 'I have a few assets. I inherited my parents' house and the boat, but their nest egg and my father's superannuation will have to go to pay off the mortgage they took out to renovate the house. But,' she paused then uttered the words she hadn't been able to make herself say, 'I will have something when I sell them both.'

'Tell me something else,' he said. 'Did you believe you were madly in love with this guy?'

Maisie folded her napkin then unfolded it and finally nodded. 'It all came at me…' She moved her shoulders. 'One moment I had my feet on the ground, the next I seemed to be flying and living and laughing again. It was extraordinary.' She pushed the napkin away.

'And how do you really feel about him now? I mean, obviously in the circumstances you've described, you'd be entitled to be angry and betrayed, but what say, hypothetically, I got him back for you?' he queried.

Maisie took an unexpected breath. 'I—I don't know. It's a bit like a dream now, and it's hard to disassociate it now from…seeing how gullible I was. But I think it would be too late to recapture the—the magic. It could only be unwillingly, if he did somehow come back now.'

'Maybe not.' He paused. 'What say he came back of his own accord because he found he couldn't forget you or live without you?'

'Do you know, I don't think I'd believe him?' she said barely audibly. 'I don't think I'd believe a word he said.' She swallowed.

'So you wouldn't take him back because of the baby?'

She hesitated. 'That wouldn't be any good, would it? If I didn't believe in him.'

He ran his fingers along the blue cut-velvet settee back and watched her narrowly. 'You don't sound especially gullible now.'

She made a steeple of her fingers then propped her chin on her fists. 'If there's one good thing that comes out of the school of hard knocks, it's that you grow up rather fast. And you suddenly begin to believe all the warnings you dismissed so lightly about falling in love and men.'

His grey eyes rested on her thoughtfully for a long moment. He'd lent her another old khaki shirt for their endeavours with the fan belt. She'd since removed it and his sister's cable-knit sweater was clean, but a little smear of grease she hadn't noticed remained under her chin.

Otherwise, completely *au naturel*, with no make-up and with her cloud of curls, she was ethereally attractive in an understated way. Her skin was pink and white and perfect. Her rosy mouth was delicate and her green eyes were stunning.

As well, as he now knew, there was a perfect little figure beneath Sonia's clothes with high, pointed breasts, a tiny waist and peachy hips.

He frowned suddenly. Why the hell he'd been moved to kiss her had been a mystery to him at the time. He had put it down to a salute for a mad act of bravery. He'd actually felt a surge of affection for her—so half drowned but still capable of yelling at him. He had regretted insulting her, but...

Had he also experienced a protective instinct?

If so, could he be falling into a trap she was building with gossamer strands around him?

Well, he decided and took the last sip of his beer, it mightn't be a bad idea to keep that in mind against any further protective urges. Because he still wasn't sure she wasn't a great little actress.

'I'm off to bed,' he said. 'How about you?'

'Yes, please.' She covered her mouth with both hands as she yawned again.

Horseshoe Bay was beautiful in the starlight.

The casuarinas along the wide curve of white beach were smudgy shadows and all the boats riding at anchor had their anchor lights reflecting in the glassy water.

Maisie was asleep in the forward berth, a comfortable cabin with two V bunks. She wore a pair of Sonia's pyjamas, a bit too big for her—and she was dreaming. Weird dreams that prompted her to do something she thought she'd grown out of—sleepwalk.

It could have been, she was to think later, a day and night full of unusual events that produced the episode, but at the time she had no idea what she was doing.

She got out of the bunk and let herself out of the cabin and up the stairs to the saloon. She walked forward and then started to climb the companionway in a slow, dreamy way. When she got to the top of the stairs she unerringly unlocked the door that led to the cockpit and was about to step outside when Rafe intervened.

He couldn't say what woke him but he got to the saloon in time to see Maisie's ghostly figure climbing the stairs. He said her name but she didn't respond so he climbed up behind her and said her name again. She didn't even turn to him.

'For crying out loud,' he murmured, 'what's this? Maisie?'

Still no response, and he realised that she was sleepwalking.

He swore softly and turned her around gently then led her down the stairs. She came unresistingly and she rested against him at the bottom.

He examined his options. There was no way he could lock her in—some stratum of her mind was capable of dealing with locks. So how was he going to stop her from getting up on deck and perhaps falling overboard?

'There's only one thing for it, Miss Wallis, I just hope to heaven you don't misinterpret it.'

He picked her up and carried her down to the double bunk in the aft berth.

She curled up with a dreamy little sigh and her eyes closed.

He watched her for a long moment then climbed in beside her and pulled the covers over them. She slept on serenely.

'Rafe! Rafe! It's Melissa and Dan. Permission to come aboard? We're coming anyway. We saw you through the binoculars from Blakesley's and wondered if you'd had trouble. Dan reckons he can help you. He must be still asleep, Dan, I'll look in the aft berth—oh!'

Rafe Sanderson shot up in bed and Maisie stirred as the cabin door opened and his friend Melissa peered in.

'Melissa!' he growled.

'I'm so sorry, Rafe,' Melissa bleated, with her eyes widening as she took in the other figure in the bed. 'I'm so—but—anyway, we'll be on deck.' She backed out hastily and closed the door.

Maisie sat up, her expression horrified and confused. She stared around and then at Rafe. 'What—why—what's *happened*?' And she started to scramble up.

He grabbed her shoulders. 'Nothing's happened, Maisie. No, listen to me,' he ordered as she tried to wriggle free. 'Absolutely nothing happened but—do you walk in your sleep?'

She froze then blinked frenetically. 'Yes. Well, I used to but it hasn't happened for a while. I thought I'd grown out of it. Do you mean…?'

He told her what she'd done and why he'd decided the only way he could keep her safe was in his bed.

She subsided. 'I did walk next door on one occasion,' she said slowly. 'And I did once find myself sitting at the bottom of the stairs in our house at Manly with no memory of how I got there or why. And, so I'm told, when I was a little kid I used to suffer night terrors.'

'Anything seem to trigger it?' he queried.

She shook her head. 'Not really, but my mother used to think I was more vulnerable to it when I was overtired.'

'You would have been overtired last night,' he said.

'Yes, probably. Oh.' Her eyes widened as she took in his ruffled hair, the green T-shirt he wore with sleep shorts, the stubble on his jaw, then she looked down at herself. 'Oh, dear, all the same, this must look…'

He released her shoulders and smoothed the collar of Sonia's pyjamas. Then he tucked her hair behind her ears. 'Extremely suspicious?' He sighed suddenly. 'I'm afraid so. Melissa is a,' he stopped and swore beneath his breath, 'a natural-born snooper and gossip. She can't help herself.'

'What will we do?' Maisie asked. 'We can only tell her the truth.'

A flash of cynicism lit Rafe Sanderson's grey eyes. 'Unfortunately, the truth is going to sound stranger than fiction.'

A stubborn little gleam entered Maisie's eyes. 'I don't care. It needs to be done.'

He shrugged after a moment. 'All right, but don't be surprised if it gets taken with a pinch of salt.'

An hour later they pulled up anchor and headed for Manly.

It was Rafe who'd made the explanations, coolly and casually, to his friends Dan and Melissa.

They'd accepted them jovially and Maisie had maintained her composure, but from the avid little gleam in Melissa's eye, quite at variance with her words, Maisie knew that Rafe had been right. There was still definitely a question mark over her and Rafe's relationship.

She flinched inwardly at the thought of it then assured herself that she was unlikely to be in either Rafael Sanderson's orbit, or his friends', for much longer, so what did it matter?

It didn't take her long to discover that it mattered greatly...

Jack Huston, Rafe Sanderson's long-suffering principal private secretary, was summoned to his boss's apartment on the Brisbane River that Sunday afternoon.

He then had the matter of Mairead Wallis briefly and succinctly explained to him.

'But—who is the guy?' he queried rather dazedly.

Rafe paced around for a moment. Then he shrugged. 'I've had some thoughts, but in the first instance I don't know if any of it is true. That's why I need to check her out.'

'Karoo and your dogs seem to suggest, well, I don't know what!'

'That may only mean she has some inside information she's got from family or staff, it could even mean she's working with someone else, some—' he gestured '—disgruntled ex-staffer.'

'What's she like?' Jack asked.

Rafe stopped pacing and directed a mocking grey glance at his secretary. 'A typical waif until she loses her temper. A— quite a character. However, if it is true someone out there is using my name to attract girls, I want to know who it is.'

'Naturally!'

'But first I want a complete background check of Mairead Wallis, commonly known as Maisie, of this address,' he handed Jack a piece of paper, 'and I would also like to know if she is pregnant.'

'You mean it might just be a ploy to get herself noticed by you?'

'I mean exactly that, Jack,' Rafe said with a cynical twisting of his lips.

'But how can I find that out?' Jack asked reasonably. 'I mean, officially find out if she's pregnant?'

'I'll leave it up to you, mate. Now, if you'll excuse me, I have another appointment but, Jack, this matter needs to be handled with utter discretion.'

'Of course,' Jack Huston assured his boss, but he blinked a couple of times before he gathered himself and left.

Rafe Sanderson's next appointment was with his mistress.

It was to have a curious outcome.

He found himself regarding the rear, naked view of his current lover.

It was a beautiful view; pale, pearly skin, gorgeous curves, a river of shiny fair hair that flowed to well below her shoulders. She was also a tall girl and, since he was six feet four, he appreciated tall girls.

The front view was just as beautiful. Deep blue eyes, a perfect oval face, more glorious curves but, he thought and stirred restlessly, not exactly an original thinker beneath all that beauty.

He was lying back, propped against some pillows on a vast bed with plum satin sheets, in a sumptuously appointed bedroom. The shades were discreetly drawn against the late-afternoon sun and his lover had just participated with him in some very sensuous, no-holds-barred sex.

But had it been so sensuous he wondered suddenly. And if not, why not?

He watched with a frown as the girl, with an elegant gesture, swept her hair up with one hand as she donned a silk robe.

Her movements were not the only elegant things about her. She dressed elegantly, she maintained this elegant apartment, she entertained elegantly and with flair. As well as that, her family owned several vast cattle stations, so there was no question of her being a fortune-huntress.

In other words, he thought drily, she would make a perfect wife, so did it matter if at times he found her—what he wondered.

A bit too perfect, a bit too suitable? A bit too compliant?

She never really surprised him. He suddenly realised that she never occupied his thoughts when he was away from her. She never annoyed him, not that he was looking for someone to annoy the life out of him, but—the admission caused him to grimace because it didn't show him in the best light even to himself—in every area other than bed, she bored him, and maybe even there now.

'Alicia,' he said suddenly, 'what would you say if I suggested we took a year off and went to sub-Saharan Africa to work amongst refugees?'

Alicia Hindmarsh turned slowly with her brush in her hand and disconcerted Rafael Sanderson for the first time.

'If you married me, Rafe, I'd say yes.' She drew her brush slowly through her fair hair.

You can't mean that, Alicia, he thought incredulously. You can't honestly believe I'm serious, anyway! Or are you saying you're prepared to pay any price to get me to marry you when you know, and I know, you'd be lucky to last a week in that kind of scenario?

'You mean you'd actually like to do that?'

'No, I'd probably hate it. There are some people who are good at that kind of thing, I don't think I'm one of them. But I would like to marry you, Rafe.'

He looked away and could have kicked himself. He might have belatedly discovered she bored him, he might find her mindset incredible, but he wasn't going to enjoy hurting her.

'I was only kidding,' he said.

'About marrying me, as well?' she asked, her big blue eyes shadowed.

'You were the one…' He stopped. 'Alicia, you'd hate being married to me; I'd make a terrible husband. For one thing I'd never be there.'

'I wouldn't mind that. I'd be perfectly happy to take you as you come.'

He took a breath and suddenly found himself on her side, although she might not realise it for what it was.

'No,' he said firmly. 'Listen to me, Alicia, don't take that kind of rubbish from any man.' He paused and realised he meant every word of it. 'Don't marry anyone, in other words, who can't live without you, whose world doesn't fall down if he can't have you because you *belong* to him and he belongs to you.'

He got out of bed and shrugged into his clothes. 'That's what you deserve, nothing less. Don't sell yourself short.'

He walked over to her and took her hand. 'Believe me.'

'Do you think you'll ever tie the knot, Rafe?' she asked.

'I…' He waved away the question. 'One day.'

'Do you know what I hope for you?'

'What?'

'You fall for someone you can't have,' she said bitterly.

He smiled lopsidedly, and kissed her hand. 'I know I deserve that. But remember what I said the next time you think you're in love, please. In fact, ask yourself this—is he good enough for *me?* If he's not, give him the flick.'

He walked home with an unpleasant taste in his mouth as a chill dusk settled.

He had no doubt he'd be the worst kind of husband for Alicia Hindmarsh. He'd walk all over her and make her life a misery. So why did he feel…regretful, yes, that was perfectly natural—but was there something else?

He frowned as he strode along the deserted inner-city pavements on a Sunday evening.

Why the hell should he find himself wondering how Maisie Wallis was spending her evening?

Why should he recall the meal they'd shared on the *Mary-Lue* last night with unexpected pleasure?

CHAPTER FOUR

MAISIE, on that Sunday evening, was making lists of everything she had to do.

Put the house on the market; ditto the boat.

That was going to entail a significant amount of sorting and cleaning, enough to keep her busy for weeks.

Find herself somewhere else to live—if only there was some way she could keep the house, she thought wistfully. But no, she was going to need the money because, apart from anything else, she was shortly going to have to give up her job.

Single mothers might be accepted in other walks of life but not at the strict private school she taught at, she knew.

That didn't mean to say she couldn't give private piano lessons and that was what she would do. But it was going to take a while to build up pupils and a reputation.

She would also shortly have to give up her part-time job with the band for obvious reasons. That reminded her, though, that she did have a ball to play at during the week.

But she suddenly pushed her lists away with a sigh and went out onto the veranda. As she leant on the railing and watched the lights in the harbour below, she thought back over the last forty-eight hours and the incredible interlude on the *Mary-Lue*.

Would she ever hear again from Rafe Sanderson she wondered.

They'd parted company in the marina car park after she'd given him her address and phone number, and received a certain Jack Huston's mobile number, his PA or something, in return.

He'd got into a sleek silver Ferrari and his last words to her, accompanied by a fleeting smile, had been, 'Take care of both of you, Maisie Wallis.'

She felt herself grow warm as she remembered the fantasies she'd experienced about the man who was not the father of her baby.

It still amazed her, she realised, to find herself capable of feeling like that about another man. She forced herself to think about it.

Of course, she acknowledged, three and a half months of the growing realisation she'd been abandoned had coloured her feelings towards the man responsible for her pregnancy. To the extent that she had got mad, and she'd even got to the stage of hating him as much as she hated the fact that she'd been so foolish.

But should she hate him entirely? Because she might have found herself rather fiercely and protectively viewing the baby she was carrying as hers, but wasn't it also always going to remind her of its father?

She sighed deeply as she contemplated the maelstrom of emotions she'd been flung into.

But she was left with two inescapable facts. What man was going to want her with another man's child?

In other words, she told herself plainly, it was no good even thinking about the real Rafe Sanderson even if he did do the strangest things to her.

The other inescapable fact was that in a little less than six months she'd be responsible for another life and—sad as it was to have happened the way it had—she *would* have someone to love.

She sniffed as some tears escaped the ban she'd placed on them and rolled down her cheeks. And she acknowledged that it was the one thought that had kept her sane, it was the thought to hold on to, a baby in her arms. It was her lifeline.

Five days later, Jack Huston reported to Rafe Sanderson on the Mairead Wallis situation.

They were in Rafe's office. It was half the size of a football field but, despite being more suitable for a luxury hotel lounge, it was the nerve centre of Sanderson Minerals and the Dixon pastoralist empire.

His boss was in his shirtsleeves with his tie loosened as he sat back in his chair and listened.

'She is pregnant—don't ask me how I got that information! I'm not proud of it.'

'You might as well tell me,' Rafe said ruefully.

Jack shrugged. 'The agency I employed put a tail on her. She happened to go to her doctor. When she came out, the receptionist made an appointment for her to have an ultrasound scan in a fortnight. I'm told this corresponds with her being roughly four months pregnant.'

Rafe half smiled. 'Go on.'

'There's absolutely nothing in her background to suggest she's a con artist of any kind. She lived with her parents until they died six months ago in an accident. She has a bachelor's degree in music, she teaches at a school renowned for its strict moral values and she plays back-up pianist in a band.'

'So she told me. What kind of a band are they and has she any particular attachment to any member?'

'No, they're all married and it seems to be a respected band, in fact, highly sought-after. She also plays once a week at a church-run retirement home—out of the goodness of her heart—and ditto at dances for a Police Youth Citizen Club.'

Rafe raised an eyebrow. 'Quite a do-gooder.'

Jack Huston paused. 'Look, the profile that emerged from people who know her is of a girl who lived a sheltered life with doting parents, a rather straitlaced girl if anything, but at the same time capable of sparkling. Reading all the reports, I formed the opinion she might have been a little unworldly and she might have been particularly vulnerable when it happened. Nor,' he added, 'is she destitute, if we're considering that as a motive for trying to attach herself to you.'

Rafe sat forward and dropped the pen he'd been toying with onto the desk. 'Go on.'

'If she sells her parents' house, which she inherited, she'll get a fairly tidy sum. It's old and needs renovation, but the position is excellent.'

Rafe brooded for a moment. 'So you are of the opinion someone using my name did take her for a ride?'

Jack lifted his shoulders. 'Yes. She's, according to all reports, well-liked, the opposite of what you'd call conniving and there's no evidence she's promiscuous. And the shock,' Jack added, 'of losing her parents was devastating, especially since they hadn't been in Queensland that long and she doesn't appear to have any other relatives.'

Jack paused for a moment then continued, 'Which could have made her particularly vulnerable to, well, whoever.'

'Yes,' Rafe mused, 'whoever. OK, thanks, Jack,' he added abruptly, 'you can leave it to me now.'

Jack Huston kept his own counsel as they prepared to move on to other business.

From his father's side, Rafe Sanderson hadn't inherited much family at all, so to speak, but the Dixon side of things was another matter.

His mother, Cecelia, had inherited the largest portion of the Dixon empire and she'd bequeathed the bulk of it to her son. That hadn't been all she'd bequeathed to him, however. She had been the eldest of six children so Rafe had also inherited "head of the clan" status of a large, often turbulent family.

Rafe bore it with equanimity, mostly, although at times he was moved to exasperation. But, as Jack well knew, in times of adversity Rafe closed ranks around the family in the way only the ultra-wealthy could.

And, thinking of the fact that Mairead Wallis had claimed there was some resemblance between the father of her baby and Rafael Sanderson, he knew that that was exactly what was going to happen now. It moved him to a feeling of pity for a girl he'd never met…

Not that he imagined her plight would be completely ignored. Within reasonable limits his boss was a fair and just man, so if her seducer came from within the family he would no doubt make some arrangements for Mairead Wallis. But if she'd ever imagined she was going to be welcomed with open arms into the bosom of the Dixon-Sanderson clan— well, he had grave doubts.

As to who her seducer was, there was a fairly strong family resemblance amongst the Dixons—Rafe himself was said to be almost a carbon copy of his Dixon grandfather—but there were also a lot of them.

'Oh,' he said, 'as for the band, they're playing tomorrow night at a dinner-dance and I believe Miss Wallis is filling in for the regular pianist, who's on holiday. Would you like me to…?'

'What kind of dinner-dance?'

'A ball really, a very posh black-tie charity "do" at the Cumberland. I believe they're still selling tickets at—' he gestured as if to say, no wonder! '—two hundred dollars a head.'

'What have I got on tomorrow night?' Rafe asked after a moment's thought.

Jack flipped through his diary. 'Uh—dinner with the McPherson-Ridges, also black-tie incidentally.'

'OK, get me a ticket to the Cumberland bash, I'll go on afterwards.'

'Just one?' Jack asked, then could have kicked himself as a cutting grey glance flew his way.

And Rafe Sanderson murmured, 'That's what I said.'

But after Jack's departure, Rafe Sanderson took a couple of minutes to gather his thoughts on Maisie Wallis.

Yes, on what he now knew to be true, perhaps she was the kind of girl who might have got herself into this situation in all innocence—he grimaced—well, got swept off her feet by someone experienced, charismatic and the rest at a time when her world was bleak and grey and lonely.

It happened.

So what was niggling him?

Wouldn't you have thought she'd be more heartbroken? Or was she more of a pragmatist than getting herself pregnant in this manner seemed to suggest?

The phone on his desk buzzed and he dismissed his thoughts, and picked it up.

Maisie made her preparations for the night's performance carefully the next afternoon.

She went to the hairdresser. Once home, she ran through Programe C on her piano, dinner music including some light classics then a gradual upping of the beat as the dancing got underway. Jim Wilson's band was nothing if not versatile and although Maisie's first musical love was the classics she was perfectly at home with whatever the band chose to play.

Then it was time to dress and, as she checked her reflection in the mirror, she was struck as she often had been before by the fact that few people might recognise this Mairead Wallis from her everyday Maisie Wallis.

"Teased out" might be how her hairdresser described her hair but what she produced was a glorious tangle of wind-swept curls that looked perfectly natural.

Then there was her make-up, stage make-up designed to enhance her features. Silver eyelids, emerald eye-liner, the strategic use of blusher, deep red lips and carefully darkened eyelashes. She'd taken some lessons when she'd first started performing.

And there was the dress. It was shocking pink, long, it moulded her figure and had a slit up the side. The bodice was encrusted with sequins, it was round-necked and sleeveless. It had also been made for her so, although it had undoubted "look at me" qualities, it was comfortable and solidly constructed.

And it somehow transformed her rather boyish little figure into a delightfully slim, willowy, more feminine outline.

Not, she paused to think, that she wasn't going to have a distinctly feminine outline shortly. In fact, it was probably lucky she'd lost some weight early on because otherwise she might not have been able to fit into this dress…

Finally, those who thought shocking pink and redheads did not go together always changed their minds when they saw Mairead Wallis wearing it.

'OK, all in place,' she murmured to herself, and donned the black velvet cloak her parents had given her. She checked her music one last time and heard the band's minibus toot. 'Coming!'

* * *

The Cumberland had turned its ballroom into a magic dell in the forest.

The tables were decked in deep rose-pink cloths with cream napkins, with real pink and cream rosebuds as their centrepieces.

There were floral streamers forming a canopy over the ballroom with an exquisite crystal chandelier at the apex of the canopy. There were silk panels against the walls, hand-painted, by the look of it, with birds and trees and butterflies. There were candles on the tables in branched silver holders.

And it was an elegant throng that streamed into the ballroom as the band played softly in the background.

Dinner suits and beautiful gowns were the order of the night. Silks and taffetas shimmered in the candlelight, lace and voile sculpted figures. Diamonds glittered and pearls glowed in gold and platinum settings. Emeralds and rubies and sapphires complemented necklines and wrists, fingers and ears—all set off beautifully against mostly black dinner suits.

'Who are these people?' Paul, the guitarist, asked *sotto voce*.

'The *crème de la crème*,' Jim replied. He played percussion and was the lead singer. 'So let's give 'em a night to remember!'

It was about midnight when Maisie thought she glimpsed Rafael Sanderson.

Dinner had been cleared away, the speeches made and the band had just played a number that had got the throng dancing their hearts out, then giving the band a breathless but ardent ovation.

Jim raised a hand for Maisie to take a bow along with the band, and she did so, several bows. Just as she was about to sit down again a tall figure with that familiar dark-blond hair caught her eye and she suffered an incredible pang of déjà vu for an instant, followed by an incredulous question—which Rafe Sanderson was it?

'Maisie?' Jim breathed.

'Oh!' She turned away and sat down hurriedly. 'Sorry. Uh—where are we?'

'Here!' He indicated her sheet music. 'Take a deep breath; you look as if you've seen a ghost.'

She swallowed. 'No, I'm fine!' And she struck a chord that led the band into some classic pop, to the crowd's further delight.

They packed up at two o'clock, an hour later than they'd planned. As they were leaving the ballroom, she felt a tap on her shoulder and looked up into the eyes of Rafael Sanderson, CEO of Sanderson Minerals.

'Can I buy you a drink?' he murmured.

Her throat worked and she closed her eyes briefly. 'That's not funny.'

He frowned. 'What do you mean?'

'That's what he said—so it was you,' she added. 'I thought for a moment, I wasn't sure—uh, no, thanks. I—'

'Perhaps I should have specified an orange juice and no seductive ulterior motives. Come.'

'Hang on, I was leaving with the band, otherwise I'll have to take a taxi and it's late anyway!'

'I'll drop you home.'

'Is—is there any news?' she asked with her eyes widening.

'No, but I need to ask you a few more things. It won't take long.'

'Maisie!' Jim called.

'Uh—Jim, it's OK, I've met a—a friend and he's going to drive me home.'

But Jim came back to be reassured and Rafe introduced himself.

'Well, I like to keep an eye on her at this time of night but if you're sure?'

'I'm sure, Jim,' Maisie said quietly. 'I probably couldn't be safer than with—Rafe.'

They found a quiet corner of the Cumberland's lounge still serving beverages and he ordered coffee, she ordered hot chocolate.

'Have you been here all night?' she queried.

'No, I came late.'

'Still, it's a bit of a coincidence, isn't it?'

'No, I knew you were playing here tonight—you're very good.'

'Thank you. I started piano lessons when I was six. Does that mean you're checking up on me in some way?'

He studied her comprehensively, the expert make-up she'd touched up only an hour ago, her hair, her lovely, rather provocative dress—and, with a twist of his lips, remembered the Maisie Wallis he'd fished out of Moreton Bay.

And he recalled with some astonishment that if it hadn't been for her hair, he mightn't have recognised her immediately tonight.

There was also her command of the piano, he thought, and the sense of rhythm that seemed to flow from her fingertips. That led him to consider her mental make-up. Of course there had to be natural talent but there must have been a lot of dedication and hard work expended to achieve her musical fluency.

Did she dance with the same fluency? he caught himself wondering out of the blue. And what would it be like to have that lovely little body in his arms, all that vitality under his direction right up close and personal? She'd been nice enough to hold fast asleep…

He grimaced and conceded that he'd proved one thing in the rather tiresome exercise he'd undertaken tonight. Most men could be forgiven for thinking Mairead Wallis, as opposed to Maisie, was sophisticated and worldly, a girl who might know the score until you got to know her better.

Then he noticed the faint blue shadows of tiredness beneath her eyes. 'I suppose so. There is quite a difference between Mairead and Maisie Wallis. But should you still be doing this?'

'I'm fine.' Maisie moved restlessly. 'There's going to be even more of a difference shortly.'

'Is that a suggestion that we get down to business?' he asked wryly.

Maisie waited as their beverages were served and she took a fortifying sip of hot chocolate. 'What is it you want to know?'

'I want to know everything he told you.'

'I can't possibly remember everything,' she protested.

'Let's start with anything to do with Karoo or the Dixon family.'

'He never mentioned the Dixon family. I—I'm not sure if he grew up on Karoo Downs, but it sounded as if he spent a lot of time there one way or another, holidays and so on. Did you? Grow up there?'

'No, but I spent a lot of time there one way or another. Could he have worked there?'

Maisie opened her mouth and closed it. 'That wasn't the impression I got, although, now that I come to think of it, there was the odd nuance of…of something…odd, something—I got the feeling there might be something uneasy…' She broke off and shook her head. 'I don't really know what it was.'

Rafe Sanderson gazed at her for a long moment in a way that was rather unnerving—as if he was looking right through her.

'So you think it could have been someone who worked there who bears you a grudge?' she asked then with her eyes widening. 'But—how does that explain the resemblance?'

He looked away at last. 'Maybe coincidence. Uh—the wedding you played at, where you first met him…can I have the details?'

She gave them to him, the date and the venue, then put a hand to her mouth. 'Why didn't I think of that?'

'You didn't realise you were dealing with an impersonator at the time?' he suggested.

'True,' she nodded, 'but now, well, he could be anyone, couldn't he?'

'Yes, but now you can leave it to me, Maisie,' he murmured. 'All right, when you've finished your chocolate, I'll take you home.' He signalled a waiter and asked for his car to be delivered to the entrance.

She drank her chocolate then looked around suddenly. 'Are you on your own?'

'Entirely.' He stood up.

'Do you usually come to balls alone?' she asked with a surprised expression.

'No, I usually do not.' He shrugged and looked bored and irritable for a moment. 'This was different, just business you could say.' He held down his hand to her.

Maisie chose to rise without his assistance, her annoyance showing clearly in the tilt of her chin and that certain glint in her eyes.

'Well, don't let me delay you any longer, Mr Sanderson,' she said evenly. 'I'm quite happy to take a taxi home; in fact, I'd rather.'

And she drew her velvet cloak around her with a flourish and picked up her music case.

'Don't be silly, Maisie,' he drawled. 'It's nearly three o'clock in the morning.'

'Oh, I'm not being silly. I'll ask the concierge to call me one and I'll only step outside when it arrives. I'll be perfectly safe.'

'What, exactly,' he said with exaggerated patience, although he shoved his hands into his pockets less than patiently, 'are you mad about now?'

'I'll tell you. You make me feel like a statistic—perhaps I am in one sense, I certainly made my mistakes—but I'm also flesh and blood and I'm dealing with…with life the best way I can. So you can write me off as an irritating, boring bit of "just business", it's up to you, but don't expect me to agree.'

'Who said anything about—?'

'You *looked* bored and irritated,' she stated.

'I got stuck at a table that was both and I'd already endured a formal dinner party,' he answered. 'It doesn't usually happen to me and I probably should have sent Jack Huston along to check out Mairead Wallis—I didn't for some reason. But *you*, as a matter of fact, were neither boring nor irritating.'

Maisie started to speak several times but she'd effectively had the ground cut away from her feet.

'Let's go,' he added.

The Ferrari was waiting for them.

They said little on the way home and he got out and escorted her to her door.

When she'd turned some lights on, he said, 'Take care again. I'll be in touch.'

She said nothing, but she watched him stride down the path, so tall and devastatingly attractive in his dinner suit.

Then she whirled herself inside, closed the door and leant back against it with her heart banging in her breast.

What had he meant? Nothing, probably. Well, as a musician, she was neither boring nor irritating—that must have been it. Unless—no, Maisie, she chided herself, you've been down this path before, *no*…

She got a call from Rafe on Sunday morning, asking her to meet him at his apartment.

'I do have some news this time,' he said. 'Can you make it at ten o'clock?'

She started to say yes then changed her mind and told him she had a standing date on Sunday mornings to play the piano at their happy hour for a retirement home. But, she said, she could meet him at twelve-thirty.

He agreed.

At twelve forty-five, Maisie buzzed his riverside apartment.

As always, her retirees had loved her Sunday happy-hour session, and as always she came away with little gifts—she had a whole collection of crochet-covered hangers and soaps and embroidered, sweet-smelling herb sachets.

She left those in her car, but carried his sister Sonia's clothes, all carefully laundered, in a holdall.

This time it was Rafe who answered the buzzer and he directed her to the penthouse suite.

As the lift bore her upwards, she did a couple of mental checks. No loss of temper was even to be entertained.

Neither was any insidious response to Rafe Sanderson's dynamic masculinity or any crazy little flutters of hope.

She stepped out right into the penthouse and took an unexpected breath. The panorama that met her eyes was breathtaking. A wide blue sky, the city and the Brisbane River wending its way around leafy Kangaroo Point and beneath the Storey Bridge.

There was a sumptuous coral-pink lounge suite that dominated the room. The walls were a darker coral and the carpet was cream. More lovely New Guinea rosewood featured in cabinets and occasional tables and some eye-catching art hung on the walls.

'Maisie,' Rafe greeted her as he rose from a settee.

But he frowned faintly because it was Mairead who'd come when he'd been expecting Maisie Wallis.

She wore a suede, amber, tulip-shaped skirt and a figure-hugging cinnamon long-sleeved knit top. Her hair was teased out and gold hoop earrings glinted through it. Her make-up was lighter than it had been a few nights ago, but subtly emphasised her eyes, the shape of her face and her mouth.

Her legs took on a new meaning in pale tights and high, slingback cream shoes. They were slender and lovely.

And he found himself wondering what exotic underwear she was wearing today…

'I ordered us lunch,' he added, belatedly as well as abruptly, and pointed to a table set for two outside on the terrace.

'Thank you,' she said quietly—truth be told, despite her mental checks and amazingly, after only a couple of days of his absence, it was a bit like a kick in the stomach to be in his presence again.

He wore light grey trousers and a black polo shirt. His belt was black leather, so were his shoes. He was shaved, she thought she detected a faint lemony cologne, and groomed—he looked every inch the powerful multimillionaire he was, and for some reason it struck a cold little chime in her heart.

Because she suddenly suspected she would cherish the

memories of the other Rafe Sanderson she'd met. Not the first one but the wet one, the unshaven one, the grease-stained one, the man with a body to die for.

But not only that, something in his manner gave rise to a premonition this might be the last time they'd meet.

She turned that set of thoughts off with a mental click and held out the holdall to him. 'Your sister's clothes. I've washed them.'

'Thanks.'

He gestured for her to proceed him onto the balcony.

She stepped through and sat down, unfurling a beige napkin.

He took the lid off a porcelain serving dish and revealed a creamy pasta dish with herbs, prawns and asparagus tips.

Maisie drew a deep breath and Rafe smiled. 'I'm with you—it smells delicious.'

But, as he dished up the pasta and sat down, his face settled into unreadable lines and once again she had the feeling they'd got onto a new, rather chilling footing.

Maisie picked up her fork and he said, 'Our quarry, the man who might have been impersonating me, could be found in Tonga. So I've made arrangements to fly out tomorrow.'

Her fork clattered to the table and her eyes nearly stood out on stalks. 'You believe me now! But—Tonga!'

'The proud Kingdom of Tonga, yes. Situated in the South Pacific just west of the international dateline.'

Maisie picked up her fork. 'What's he doing there?'

He ate for a moment then sat back. 'That remains to be seen.'

'Well, who is he? And how do you know about him?'

Rafe hesitated. 'That's classified information at the moment.'

Maisie stared at him with her lips parted. 'Hang on, this could be the father of my baby! You can't keep that as classified information from me!'

He smiled drily. 'Actually, I can until I've verified things, but rest assured, if this is the guy, I'll make the appropriate decisions on your behalf. In other words, Maisie, you can leave it up to me now.'

Maisie fought a pitched, private battle with herself and, for once in her life, won it. To contradict him angrily was not the way to go, not with this businesslike man who looked almost frighteningly capable of getting his own way.

Anyway, if she lost the battle she'd be left with no clues as to what this actually signified, this disengagement, but she had the strong feeling it meant something that might not be beneficial to her...

'Well, that's a relief,' she said. 'So—how will you get to Tonga?'

'The company jet.'

She made a face. 'How does a normal person get to Tonga?'

His eyes rested on her face in a rather narrowed, probing way then he said, 'From Brisbane you have to fly via Nadi in Fiji or via Sydney. There aren't daily flights, so it can be a time-consuming business.'

'I've always thought it sounded rather fascinating—lucky you! It's a bit surprising, though, that you've got the time to do this.' She said it rather whimsically but in fact her mind was racing.

'I'll be able to combine it with some business. I've been there several times before. In fact, I've sailed the *Mary-Lue* there, to the Vava'u group of islands. They have the finest natural harbour in the South Pacific.'

'How wonderful,' she enthused. 'Tell me about it.'

So he did as they finished their lunch. About the marvellous volcanic and coral isles of Vava'u, about Tongatapu, the main island of Tonga and Nuku'alofa, the capital. About the pigs that wandered freely and the people who still often wore traditional garb—a woven palm mat tied round their middle over their clothes, and the choir singing in the local churches that was awesome. And above all the warmth of the local people.

'I'm green with envy,' she said. 'So, I suppose there's nothing more for me to do at the moment, but you will get in touch when you get back, won't you?'

'Of course.'

She put her napkin on the table then appeared to be struck by another thought. 'How will I be able to get in touch with you in case I need to?'

'You won't need to while I'm in Tonga,' he said definitely.

'No, I suppose not. But when you get back?'

'Use the number I gave you, Jack Huston's, but I promise you I'll be in touch.'

At that moment his own mobile rang and he pulled it out of his pocket, excused himself and got up to walk to the veranda railing.

'Yes, Jack,' he said into it. 'Have you got the flight plan? OK. Book me into The Tongan Beach Resort for two nights—Tuesday, Wednesday, I'll handle things from there. See you.' He disconnected and turned back to her. 'Well, Maisie, I'm sorry to end our lunch a bit abruptly but I have another appointment shortly.'

Maisie controlled her emotions brilliantly. She allowed none of her *Oh, no you don't, Rafael Sanderson!* emotions to show.

She stood up and said casually, 'Well, thanks for lunch. Don't forget I'm relying on you to sort this out! Oh, and enjoy Tonga.'

He didn't respond immediately because for one instant, as he watched her, so pretty in her smart outfit but a different sort of girl and plucky with it, he was tempted to spurn his advice to himself.

He knew he should forget the memory of her cuddled against him so sweet and trusting and lovely. Forget her poised, unusually attractive Mairead persona and the odd little thought that came with it—she could take her place anywhere.

Forget the fact that she was never boring to be with…

Because he could only further complicate her already complicated life.

And if that doesn't work, he advised himself drily, remember she is carrying another man's baby…

Not to mention the complications of who the bastard going round impersonating him could be, which was another good reason to take this tack.

'My pleasure,' he murmured, and started to walk her towards the lift. 'I know I've said this before but look after yourself—and I mean properly,' he added.

Was she imagining it, she wondered, or was there an air of finality to those words?

No, she decided, she wasn't imagining it.

The lift arrived and she stepped in and waved at him, quite sure he never intended to deal with her in person again, never to know that she had other ideas.

She went straight home and got on to her computer. While she was waiting for websites to load, she realised she was still magnificently angry, not only because she refused to be brushed aside like this, but also because she wasn't a fool.

It had become as clear as crystal to her that Rafe Sanderson knew the man who'd taken such advantage of her and could well have decided to protect him.

How he knew had also become clear the more she thought about it. He must have somehow got the guest list from the wedding she'd been playing at, but, while it would have meant nothing to her, one of those names on it must have meant something to him.

Take it a step further and recall the resemblance between the two men and it could only mean they were related…

There could be no other reason for keeping that name from her as classified information. No other reason for a man to take three days out of his busy schedule to track someone down in the wilds of the South Pacific.

Her eyes widened as she brought up The Tongan Beach Resort—it was on Vava'u. Bingo, she thought. But how to get to the fabulous group of islands without it taking for ever or breaking the bank?

She was almost cross-eyed when she came up with a flight from Brisbane to Fiji that connected reasonably with a direct flight, a new service, to Vava'u.

She sighed with relief, goggled a bit at the price, but she had started a holiday fund and could pay the balance in instalments on her credit card—she just hadn't anticipated going to Tonga, but the more she saw of it, the more enchanted she was.

She made the booking that would see her arrive in Vava'u the following evening. Then she scrolled through the accommodation options and found the Backpacker's Hostel in Neiafu, the capital of Vava'u. It wasn't possible to book online immediately, she discovered, but at least she knew of the existence of cheap accommodation.

Finally she sat back and felt some of her anger drain away and some consternation seep in, in its place. Had she let her temper run away with her?

She shrugged. She was as much, if not more entitled to find out who had been impersonating Rafe Sanderson; that was what it boiled down to and no one could tell her any different.

But how did the real Rafe Sanderson fit into it all? For her?

'An impossible dream,' she answered herself quietly, 'but it's shattered now, anyway.'

Yes, she couldn't deny the attraction that had sprung up for her, so surprisingly, out of a heart that she'd thought had been turned to stone and at the last time in her life that it should have happened to her.

Perhaps it had started life as a slender shoot brought to life by the fact that he'd made her feel safe and not only in his arms after rescuing her?

Perhaps it was compounded by the fact that he was the only person, apart from her doctor, who knew?

At least someone, she thought, had taken into account the vagaries of pregnancy and made her feel looked after, however briefly. He'd also divined how she felt about this baby…

Was it only natural she'd felt *something* for him?

On the other hand she knew so little about him, it was wildly insane even to think of him in any other terms than as a man who had briefly been kind to her.

And now she was angry with him. Now she didn't know how far she could trust him. Who was to say, for example, his impersonator wasn't a married man? If so, and he was family, he would have all the resources at Rafe Sanderson's disposal—and she had no doubt they were formidable—close ranks around him.

Would she even get a name?

She pulled a tissue from the box on the desk and blew her nose.

But the thing is, Maisie, she told herself, that's not the point.

The point is—there are several.

No man, least of all Rafe Sanderson who could have anyone, is going to want you, pregnant with another man's child.

Why do I have to keep reminding you of that? she asked herself with a touch of impatience.

But the most important point of all is that you have to stop bobbing around like a cork, emotionally and in every other sense. You have to set goals and if you firmly believe a child deserves to know who its father is, this is the way to go.

She packed carefully that night.

She was an organised traveller and used to travelling light.

Then she looked through her small jewellery bag and took out her mother's gold signet ring. It was like a lucky charm for her and she always wore it when she was away, sometimes on her left hand, where, when it was turned under, it looked like a wedding band. It had proved handy on several occasions to protect her from men on the prowl.

For some reason, she put it straight onto her left hand for her trip to Tonga…

CHAPTER FIVE

MAISIE noticed the sleek, fast-looking jet on the tarmac as she disembarked a little stiffly from her flight at Lupepau'u Airport on the main island of the Vava'u group.

But the light had faded and anyway, all it bore was a logo she didn't recognise. Nor was she expecting to encounter Rafe Sanderson until the following day. She was unaware that he'd amended his booking at The Tongan Beach Resort to include that night, Monday.

Therefore, she nearly died of fright when a hand descended onto her shoulder and a familiar voice said her name incredulously and swore audibly.

She turned and there he was, as tall and as impressive as he'd ever been, from his thick short hair, a yellow T-shirt and khaki trousers down to his boots. As lean and strong and beautiful as ever, but—she went pale at the blaze of fury in Rafe Sanderson's grey eyes as he scanned her from head to toe.

He registered her jeans and boots, her denim jacket over a pink blouse, her hair tied back into a pony-tail but escaping it. He scanned the backpack on a frame she'd collected from the luggage area and her shoulder bag.

'What the hell are you doing here?' he growled.

'I...I,' she stammered and swallowed. 'I have just as much right to be here as you do.'

'I told you I would deal with this,' he ground out.

She stiffened. 'It's how you intend to deal with it that bothers me— Oh!' She realised there was a gap in the queue in front of her and she moved forward.

'What do you mean?' he shot at her as she turned back to him.

'I mean I formed the distinct impression that you may know the man who fathered my baby and may even be going to protect him somehow!'

He didn't precisely deny it. His eyes narrowed as he said tersely, 'What gave you that idea?'

'I wasn't born yesterday!' She tossed her head proudly as her eyes glinted angrily. 'Furthermore, I can't be shoved aside while you—close ranks.'

'If you've quite finished?' he queried smoothly.

'Actually, I could think of a lot more to say, but this isn't the time or place.' She tilted her chin at him.

He half smiled. 'In the meantime, it's your turn.' He gestured.

She blinked then clicked her tongue exasperatedly to see she'd reached the Customs officer who was waiting for her.

She heaved her backpack onto the counter and handed in her entry card, upon which she'd clearly documented the fact that she had nothing to declare.

The customs officer politely enquired if he might check?

Maisie agreed and had to suffer a full check of her baggage that displayed her personal items, including a green bra and knickers with frangipanis on them, to public view.

She refused to look at Rafe Sanderson, standing right beside her, but a tinge of pink entered her cheeks.

If that wasn't bad enough, once she was waved through and was repacking her bag, Rafe sailed through his own encounter with Customs without getting his bags inspected—he was even greeted like a long-lost friend.

This caused her to mutter irritably beneath her breath, and caused him to laugh softly.

'If you could see your face, Maisie. Here, allow me.'

Her backpack had wheels and she was perfectly capable of handling it, but she only just restrained herself from indulging in a small, undignified battle for control of it as he took it over.

'I'm staying at the Backpacker's Hostel,' she said definitely, however, 'and I'll make my own way there.'

'Have you booked?'

'No, but—'

'You may stay where you like,' he countered, 'but I have a car and a driver organised, and, since we'll be passing the place, you might as well come with me.'

At that moment, a beaming Tongan bearing a placard with the name Sanderson printed on it approached and introduced himself as Rafe's driver.

'Welcome back, Rafe!' he enthused and his eyes fell on Maisie and went unerringly to her left hand, where her mother's signet ring had slipped round so only the gold band was showing.

Rafe followed his glance. He hadn't noticed the ring before, and he raised his eyebrows.

But the driver did more. He came to an entirely wrong conclusion. 'Could this be Mrs Sanderson?' he enquired joyfully. 'Welcome, ma'am—oh, this is a real pleasure. I'm James.' He held out his hand.

'First names are important to Tongans,' Rafe murmured audibly only to Maisie.

'I—I,' Maisie stammered, taking the hand, 'I'm Maisie, James; lovely to meet you, but—'

'Well, let's get this show on the road,' James overrode her. 'My car awaits you. This way!' And he turned away, taking Maisie's bag from Rafe.

'Do something!' Maisie urged Rafe.

'James,' Rafe said and paused. 'Incidentally, James, what's the accommodation situation on Vava'u like at the moment?'

James turned back. 'Thanks to this new direct connection from Fiji and a wonderful whale season, I do believe we're booked out. I know the Backpacker's Hostel is full to over-flowing, all the accommodation in Neiafu is pretty much the same, and most of the islands! Just as well you have a reser-vation, Rafe and Maisie!'

The trip into Neiafu was tense—for Maisie.

She'd climbed into the backseat of James' car, expecting Rafe to follow her, but he closed her door courteously and got into the front, where he and James started to chat.

As they drove through the darkened, mostly unpopulated landscape, her mind seethed. How was she going to get herself out of this? Just come out and tell James he'd made a mistake?

But although she opened her mouth to do it a couple of times, something held her back. What if there was no accom-modation available?

She swallowed. She might be a seasoned traveller, but the prospect of finding a beach or a bench in a completely strange country she hadn't seen in the daylight was not a pleasant one.

Then they rolled into Neiafu. As they drove through at a sedate forty kilometers per hour, she could see the *No Vacancy* signs sprinkled through the little town. In fact, the first one she saw was on the Adventure Backpacker's Hostel board.

She sat back and bit her lip. Then she tuned into Rafe's con-versation with James. James was explaining that Tongan

Beach Resort had come under new management recently but it was still a fine establishment, and Rafe would recognise many of the staff.

'And this news,' he added and turned briefly to Maisie, 'will bring them much joy!'

Maisie sat back under the sensation of feeling totally sandbagged.

'At least it's got single beds.'

Maisie stood in the middle of the room they'd been allotted, in a low, bungalow-style block of four rooms with verandas, and dropped her shoulder bag onto one of the beds.

She'd somehow survived the "joy" with which she and Rafe had been greeted—no one seemed to give it the least thought that the room had been booked in one name only. No forms had had to be signed, no one had asked to see their passports.

She'd digested the news that now The Tongan Beach Resort was full!

She'd survived the embarrassment caused by the staff when, to their genuine consternation, they'd realised the last room available had single beds. They offered to change them to a double bed, but Rafe had declined.

She looked around. It was pleasant and comfortable. The walls were painted a delicate apricot and there was a dado running around the room made of tapa, a bark fabric with traditional Tongan painting and symbols on it.

The floor was tiled, there was a cane setting of two chairs and a glass-topped table, and on each bed with its colourful cover there was a fluffy white towel decorated with a hibiscus bloom.

'I suppose so,' she said wearily.

He came to stand in front of her. 'There was nothing else to do, Maisie.'

She twisted her fingers together and his gaze dropped to her mother's ring.

'Incidentally, why *are* you wearing a wedding ring?'

'I'm not.' She explained about the ring. 'I'd completely forgotten I was wearing it on my left hand.'

He shoved his hands in his pockets. 'In the circumstances—protecting the local sensibilities, not to mention my reputation—it might have been a good idea.'

'No, look, somehow we have to end this farce—'

'Maisie,' his eyes hardened, 'this is another perfect example of leaping before you look. You'd never have got stranded on the *Mary-Lue* otherwise and you've done the same thing again!'

'But—'

'No buts,' he ordered. 'It's not my fault the place is booked out and what did you expect me to do? Abandon you?'

Maisie bit her lip. 'Well, no—and thanks for that, I mean, really, but masquerading as your wife is…' She trailed off helplessly.

'It's done now,' he said tersely. 'And we'll be getting out of Tonga as soon—as soon as I've sorted things out. Besides which,' he added with a lethal little smile, 'we've already spent a night together from which,' he paused as she opened her mouth, but the look in his eyes was so quelling she shut it again, 'from which,' he continued, 'despite cuddling up to me as if it came naturally, you emerged completely unscathed.'

'I didn't cuddle up!'

'Oh, yes, you did,' he contradicted.

To her mortification she went bright scarlet. 'I—well, I apologise. I had no idea. I don't know what made me—'

'I do. You'd had a long, traumatic day, you were overtired, your mind was playing tricks on you—and you are pregnant.'

She could come up with absolutely nothing to refute this.

He smiled drily. 'OK, here's what I suggest. Have a shower while I go and order dinner. Is there anything you don't eat?'

She shook her head.

He glanced at his watch. 'We still have time but don't be too long, there's a good girl.' And he strolled out of the sliding glass doors.

Maisie watched him go with a sudden little glint of fire in her eyes, then she stepped across and drew the curtains closed with something of a snap.

The *en suite* bathroom was modern and gleaming white and the shower was steaming hot.

She had to admit when she emerged, glowing, from it that she felt better. She pulled on her clean best jeans and her silky knit black top with silver studs. She pushed her feet into a pair of sandals and she rubbed her hair almost dry, then ran her hands through it several times until she was satisfied with it.

She moisturised her face and hesitated briefly. Then she applied some lip gloss, some silvery green eye-shadow and brushed on some mascara. It was during these ministrations that she realised she was starving and that gave her further impetus to leave the room and continue her masquerade as Rafe Sanderson's wife.

She stopped dead for several moments a few feet from the veranda.

In all her earlier confusion she'd taken little in about the resort, but now, by the light of a full moon, the magic of it hit her.

The graceful palm trees, the beach almost on the doorstep, the white day-night lilies that lined the sandy pathways and the palm-thatched dining room with its shutters open to reveal the gleam of candlelight, the glint of polished glassware and the glorious aroma of food...

Rafe was waiting for her at a table for two. He'd ordered a glass of red wine for himself and a lemon, lime and bitters for her.

He rose to pull out her chair and, as she sank into it, he told her that he'd ordered fillet steak in a mushroom sauce for them. 'Sound OK?' he added.

Maisie hesitated then had to smile ruefully. 'I feel as if I could demolish a whole cow.'

He laughed and she looked around. There were only three couples still dining.

'It's very nice,' she murmured and sipped her drink.

'Yes,' he agreed.

She hesitated, remembering her resolve made in a flash of anger a short time ago, to refuse to allow herself to be treated like a naughty schoolgirl. But how to implement it? Get a conversation going that would show him she was a lot more mature than he gave her credit for?

She said the first thing that came into her head. 'Are you musical?'

He thought for a moment. 'No more than most. I can hold a tune, I can dance, but I can't play anything. You—have the edge over me in that, Maisie.'

She looked amused. 'Not much of an edge. But,' she smiled openly, 'it's nice to know it's there.'

He rubbed his jaw. 'You're actually looking for some edge over me?'

'Yes.'

'Why?'

'Oh, damn,' she laughed ruefully, 'it hasn't come out quite as I planned. I mean—I didn't mean to admit it. I meant to show you through my informed conversation, my poise et cetera, et cetera, that I should not be treated like an irresponsible child. And,' she added with a suddenly straight little look, 'to have it remembered that I do have every right to be here.'

He grimaced. 'You wanted to put me in my place well and truly?'

She pursed her lips. 'I did. I have to tell you I've been angry and upset ever since you gave me the brush-off in Brisbane.'

He rubbed the bridge of his nose. 'I should have known,' he murmured ruefully. 'I not only saw you jump into Moreton Bay, I fished you out. Well, my apologies, Maisie, I was in the wrong.'

She stared at him wide-eyed. 'Do you really mean that?'

His eyes were wickedly amused. 'Are you asking me to cross my heart and hope to die? Consider it done.'

She blinked, and their steaks arrived. She closed her eyes in appreciation of the divine aroma that rose from her plate. 'Maybe it's food!' she said and her lashes flew up.

He looked into her green eyes. 'Food?'

'It's quite impossible for me to stay angry with *anyone* in the presence of food, especially given this marvellously delectable meal in front of me.'

He laughed and murmured, 'I'll remember that. You'd better tuck in.'

From then on, conversation just seemed to come naturally to them. He asked about her parents and she told him something of her earlier life on a variety of army bases and the only shadow came when she told him about losing them.

She even glowed a little as he laughed at some of her reminiscences, but, once, she did ask herself what she thought she was doing. She had been distinctly annoyed with him for landing her in this situation, even if she had contributed to it. She still didn't know whom he might be shielding.

But the questions disappeared from her mind because she simply couldn't stop enjoying herself…

Halfway through a deliciously decadent dessert, she started to yawn.

'Uh-oh,' he said with a wry little smile.

'What does that mean?' she queried.

'It means—when you need to sleep, you need to curl up like a cat.'

She shrugged. 'It's been a long day, but I've always been a good sleeper. When, that is, I'm not sleepwalking. No, just joking,' she added as he frowned, 'it's only happened at rare intervals. I'm quite sure I'm safe tonight. Or rather, *you're* quite safe tonight.' A sparkle of humour lit her eyes.

He smiled perfunctorily and, despite her weariness, Maisie detected that the air had suddenly become threaded with tension between them as his grey gaze remained on her.

She was not to know that he'd been in a position to take in the reaction, of the other couples dining, to her arrival in the dining room.

She herself hadn't registered the fact that all six people, men and women, had taken a second look.

She'd had no idea that her black top particularly suited her, that her tangle of curls was breathtaking and the make-up she'd applied had added the gloss to a highly desirable girl, now glowing in her second trimester of pregnancy…

She didn't realise that Rafe Sanderson was thinking some rather grim thoughts along the lines of—safe from her?

That was becoming highly debatable because it was becoming increasingly difficult to divorce Mairead Wallis from the infuriated waif he'd fished out of the water. It was becoming increasingly obvious that he not only felt protective, but more…

Above all, though, how the hell could he spend another night, even in a separate bed, chastely with her when the stirring of his body told him he wanted her? Wanted to run his fingers through her curls and down her body, that smooth pink- and-white lovely little body. And that he rather urgently needed to see the reaction in those green eyes to the things he did to her, to test his suddenly-formed theory that he could make her sparkle in the act of love—for him alone?

He moved restlessly.

'What have I done now?'

He came out of his amazing thoughts to see her watching him a little nervously.

He shrugged. 'Nothing. But here's what I suggest: I might have a nightcap in the bar while you take yourself to bed.'

Maisie blinked and examined the feeling that she'd been metaphorically slapped in the face. Then she closed her eyes and castigated herself for being ridiculous. It was the obvious answer for two people sharing a room in the circumstances they were. So why did she feel chilled and shut out?

She folded her napkin and put it on the table. 'Good idea. Incidentally, when are you going to tell me what you know— about things? I mean, now I'm here, you might as well.'

There was a cool silence, then he said abruptly, 'Tomorrow, Maisie. Goodnight. Sleep well.' He stood up.

She had no option but to follow suit. She murmured 'Goodnight' and made her way back to the room.

But she stopped halfway and looked up at the moon, and was struck by a feeling of loneliness that nearly took her breath away…

* * *

She tossed and turned for over an hour but he didn't come.

She wondered what impression this would make on the staff. A reluctant husband? How ironic was that?

She wondered about all sorts of things. She'd set out on this trip full of a crusading spirit on her baby's behalf, not to mention full of righteous indignation.

Then, under the influence of his company, she'd forgotten all about that until she'd been brought rather sharply back to earth by him.

But had it been even worse than that? she asked herself.

Had she given off the vibes of a girl who fancied Rafe Sanderson because she just couldn't help herself? Was that why he'd decided to shut a metaphorical door in her face?

The thought was mortifying and made her feel helpless and confused. It also presaged a feeling of doom as she remembered that attack of loneliness she'd suffered in the moonlight…

Would she ever get over Rafe Sanderson?

No, no, it could hardly have come to that yet, she assured herself. Even if she couldn't stop herself from loving his company, even if she felt so restless and unloved, yearning, even burning a little to be loved…

She finally fell asleep with it all going round and round in her head.

When she woke the next morning she realised she hadn't heard him come to bed although his bed had been slept in. But there was no sign of him.

Instead, there was a note on the pillow.

She reached for it groggily. It said,

Something's come up; I'll be gone until tomorrow morning. I've booked you on a whale-watching cruise— have fun. I think we'll be going home tomorrow. Rafe.

She lay back and closed her eyes. She thought about how she'd sparkled last night in his company, quite unwittingly but, perhaps, quite revealingly. And now this.

Yet another disengagement. Could the message be louder or clearer? He didn't want anything more to do with her.

CHAPTER SIX

AT FIVE o'clock that afternoon, Maisie came back from her whale-watching cruise in a much better frame of mind than when she'd set out.

Hard not to be, she reasoned, on a glorious day when she'd got to within metres of three humpback whales—a mother, a day-old calf and an escort—for the islands of Vava'u were right in the path of the annual whale migration north from the Antarctic.

She did have one regret. The stronger swimmers of the party had actually snorkelled in the crystal-clear Pacific waters with the giants but she'd, at the last minute, changed her mind about it although she was a good swimmer. But it had been made clear to everyone that they did so at their own risk.

'I'm pregnant,' she told the girl guide, 'so maybe I shouldn't.'

'If they suddenly start to breach and you have to get away fast it can be really strenuous, so no, I wouldn't,' the girl agreed. 'It's also not that easy to get back on the boat in a hurry. But you could probably snorkel later at the Swallow Caves.'

So with that Maisie had had to be content, and it had still been a unique experience.

Once the swimmers were back on board the boat, their

three whales had put on a magnificent display of breaching, propelling themselves backwards out of the water in an arc, and flapping the water with their tails. The calf had copied everything its mother and escort did and was especially endearing, looking so small against the other two.

Maisie decided it was an emotional experience that actually brought a lump to her throat, and she discovered that her fellow cruisers, all from the resort, felt the same.

She didn't realise amidst all the clicking cameras as everyone photographed the whales that one of the cameras was trained on her as much as the whales.

She failed to notice that one of the guests, a man in his late twenties who'd actually been in the dining room the night before but had left before she and Rafe had, was studying her curiously from time to time and he continued to do so throughout the day.

She had no idea that he'd heard her tell the guide she was pregnant.

After that they'd cruised around the islands, stopped on a perfect white beach for lunch and finally snorkelled in the fabulous Swallow Caves.

Their boat dropped them off on the Tongan's jetty and she was still exhilarated as she walked to the room. She even stopped to look around affectionately at the Tree House built on stilts over the beach and used for private dinners, at the red-gold leaves of the cotton-wood trees that lined the beach, the Sand Bar with its beach-sand floor, the distinctive shape of the palm thatch roof of the dining room.

But then it hit her that she was the only one alone, all the others were couples, and she didn't even have anyone to describe her wonderful day to.

She closed herself sadly into her room, actually dabbing

at a couple of stupid tears, to find Rafe stretched out on his bed, but awake with his hands crossed behind his head.

He sat up as she dropped her holdall in her surprise.

'You!' she gasped.

He sat up and frowned. 'Yes, me. What's wrong?'

'N-nothing,' she stammered. 'I mean, I'm all sandy and salty, some of it must have got in my eyes, and I really need a shower, but—that's all.'

He got up and came over to her. 'You looked as if you were crying.' He shrugged as he inspected her closely. 'How was your day?'

Relief flooded Maisie and her face lit up with genuine enthusiasm. 'Absolutely marvellous. I didn't actually swim with the whales—'

'Why not? Oh,' he added as Maisie looked down at her stomach, 'of course. Well, at least you're acquiring some wisdom along those lines.'

'Yes and thanks so much for organising it—it was still wonderful! But,' she paused, 'I wasn't expecting you until tomorrow.'

'Change of plans,' he said. 'Why don't you have a quick shower? Are you particularly starving?'

'No, I had a big lunch on the boat so I can wait for dinner, but—'

'I'll wait outside,' he interrupted.

Maisie showered and changed into khaki shorts and a loose primrose blouse. She tied her hair back and slid her sandals on.

Rafe got up as she let herself out onto the veranda. 'Let's go for a walk,' he murmured.

She looked surprised then shrugged and fell into step beside him.

They walked to the main entrance, a set of gates with a

fence climbing the hillside on one side and a rock wall groyne extending into the sea on the other. At the end of the groyne was a little thatched hut with wooden seats.

As they approached the gates, a man got out of a car parked on the other side and opened the gate—and Maisie suddenly stopped dead.

Rafe stopped, too, and watched her intently as all colour left her face and her mouth worked. Then she blinked and closed her eyes experimentally and, as her lashes fluttered up, she said in a trembling voice, 'R-rafe? I mean…'

'No,' the man beside her side said on a harsh breath. 'It's my cousin, Tim Dixon.' He took hold. 'Maisie, here's what I suggest. That you and Tim discuss things in the hut. I'll leave you alone. But I've booked the Tree House for dinner and you and I can—talk.'

He turned on his heel and walked away.

Some time later Maisie stood on the beach on her own, staring blindly out to sea but with the sensation that the scales had fallen from her eyes.

Tim Dixon did bear quite a resemblance to his cousin and he'd admitted to impersonating Rafe. As he'd done so, she'd glimpsed a biting hostility towards Rafe.

But why? she'd asked.

He'd shrugged and told her that Rafe had a lot more than he deserved, a lot that was rightly his, Tim Dixon's.

He wouldn't bore her with too many details, he'd gone on to say but, he'd added with a charming smile, the irony of the fact she was one girl who apparently had never heard of Rafe Sanderson hadn't failed to strike him.

Maisie had been struck dumb.

Then he'd sobered and told her some of his background.

He'd also said he had nothing to offer her, he was on his uppers with a string of debts around his neck, that was why he was in Tonga working as a diving instructor, but he would acknowledge he was the baby's father.

Throughout it all, along with his golden good looks—his hair was bleached fairer by the sun and was now longer, and a pair of board shorts and a T-shirt showed off his tan as well as his physique—she'd got bewildering flashes of the man who had swept her off her feet.

But as he spoke, even sometimes with the wry humour, the charm and the whimsy she'd loved, the knowledge had grown in her heart that Tim Dixon was like a rogue leopard, beautiful, mesmerising, but a loner with only his best interests at heart.

She hadn't said much at all.

She hadn't given him a piece of her mind or called him any of the hard names he deserved.

She'd agreed that there was no point in pursuing a paternity suit, but at that point he'd really stunned her when he told her Rafe would make some settlement on her anyway.

But you hate him, she'd cried then.

He'd agreed coolly.

That was when she'd stumbled to her feet and walked away from him.

But he'd had the nerve to call out, 'So it's settled, Maisie?'

'Yes. Just go away!'

That was why she stood on the beach for so long with her sandals in her hand, viewing everything that had happened to her through new eyes.

Then she turned to go back to the room, but one of the waitresses called out to her as she passed the dining room, to tell her Rafe was waiting for her in the Tree House and she was just about to serve the first course.

It was a still, perfect night and the candle flames in the thatched Tree House hardly wavered as the water lapped softly on the beach below.

Rafe had changed into jeans and a blue shirt and he rose as she appeared. After taking one look at her face, he poured her a glass of wine.

'No,' she murmured.

'Yes.' He put the glass in her hand. 'One glass is not going to hurt you. I'm sorry I did it that way but I wanted you to be sure I wasn't covering anything up.'

'I don't think however you did it would have made any difference.' She sniffed and licked some salty tears from her lips. Then she looked across at him bravely. 'How did you work it out?'

He looked away briefly. 'Right from the start Tim was at the back of my mind. We have been mistaken for each other occasionally. He does bear me a grudge.'

'But you didn't tell me—'

'Maisie,' he interrupted, 'I didn't know for sure it was Tim, but if it was, I had no way of knowing you weren't in cahoots with him.'

She digested this with widening eyes, but in light of the revelations she'd so recently been party to, she had to concede he had a point.

'How did you get him to agree to acknowledge the baby?'

'Don't ask.' He rubbed his jaw. 'So?'

'He said—' She stopped as she heard the waitress climbing the stairs. The first course she brought was asparagus soup.

'He said?' Rafe prompted as she left them alone.

'He said that he had good cause to bear you a grudge. That you'd inherited what he should have and he'd had to grow up in your shadow and he'd had to—grin and bear it.'

Rafe picked up his spoon. 'It had nothing to do with me. Tim's father was my mother's brother. In the natural course of events he would have inherited the Dixon empire. But he fell out with his father, my grandfather—he was caught red-handed siphoning off profits, and worse—and disinherited. Most if it went to my mother as the oldest child, and all the others were girls. Eat something, Maisie.'

She crumbled the roll on her plate and tasted the asparagus soup; it was delicious but she had no appetite, although she forced herself to take a few spoonfuls.

'Then,' Rafe went on, 'Tim's father, my uncle, died in a parachuting accident when Tim was about six. My mother took pity on Tim, and his mother, and she brought them into the family; my grandfather had died by then. She paid for Tim's schooling and university and she set up a trust fund for him and his mother. And he and I did spend a lot of time together at Karoo as we grew up.'

'Did you realise how much he resented you?' Maisie asked.

Rafe looked out over the darkened water for a long time. 'He kept it to himself until my mother died. We were in our mid-twenties. Then he dropped a bombshell—that he intended to sue me for what he claimed was his rightful inheritance.'

Maisie put her spoon down and pushed her soup away and took a sip of wine.

'It was settled out of court,' Rafe went on. 'Not that we felt he had any leg to stand on, particularly since it was my father and a lot of Sanderson money that had saved the Dixon empire from collapse because of drought and low wool prices by then—something Tim wasn't aware of.'

Rafe finished his soup and reached for his wine. He swirled his glass and looked down at the pale gold depths before looking at Maisie. 'But we decided to make Tim a settlement on the condition that he made no more claims. He agreed. Sad to say,' Rafe paused, 'it looks as if he's gone through that, as well as the trust.'

Tears brimmed, causing Maisie's green eyes to sparkle in the candlelight. 'It wouldn't—it wouldn't have been easy for him, though.'

Rafe studied her and thought his own thoughts. Was she still a little in love with his cousin? His mouth tightened briefly.

'Does that mean you want him back?' he asked abruptly.

'Oh, no.' Maisie shook her head.

'It sounds as if you're feeling sorry for him, all the same,' he pointed out.

'No.' Maisie cupped her face and propped her elbows on the table. What had she meant? she wondered. It fell into place unexpectedly. She wanted some mitigating circumstances for the father of her baby. Some way not to think of him with utter bitterness and contempt because he was going to be a part of her baby, whether she liked it or not. But how to explain that?

She sighed. 'No. It's over.'

'Tim Dixon,' Rafe said slowly, 'can be irresistible, until you really get to know him.'

'Thank you,' she whispered.

They were on their next course, fish of the day which happened to be delectable fresh-caught wahoo, when Maisie started to feel a little less traumatised and able to think of other things.

'So I guess this is the end of the line for us,' she murmured.

'Maisie.' He paused.

She allowed her gaze to roam over him briefly, taking in the angles and shadows of his face, as he appeared to debate internally with himself. Not only was it a good-looking face, but it could also be alight with intelligence, breathtakingly attractive when he laughed and frustratingly enigmatic in repose as you wondered how really to reach this man.

Plus there were the lean, strong lines of his broad shoulders beneath his shirt, his long, lovely hands—and she felt an awful pang in her breast because there might not be many more occasions for her to feast her eyes on Rafe Sanderson.

If she wasn't for him, and she knew she could never be—how could he ever forget, how could she ever forget she was carrying another man's child, and not only that, but also whose child it was. He touched something within her that, she now realised, Tim Dixon had never touched.

What a time and what a way to find it out, she thought.

'Maisie,' he said as if he'd rethought what he'd been going to say moments ago, 'where will you live? You said something about selling your parents' house.'

Surprise caused her to blink, and, she was to realise later, caused her to answer incautiously, 'I'd love to be able to stay on in the house. I don't feel so lonely there now as I first did and it brings back—' she tipped her head '—memories I cherish. But it's not possible, so I'll probably rent a place once it's sold, where I can give piano lessons.'

He carefully dissected a piece of fish and removed a bone. 'You will be able to stay on. I'll make it possible.'

Maisie put down her knife and fork as the implication sank in and she remembered Tim Dixon's words that had so incensed her...

'No, I don't want anyone's charity, let alone yours,' she said.

He raised an eyebrow at her. 'Let alone mine?'

'I—I…' She couldn't go on.

'Why particularly not mine, Maisie?'

She read the determination in his eyes to get an answer.

'B-because—because I need to get away from all this. I need to be able to put it all behind me and make a fresh start. I—'

'Who said anything to the contrary?' he queried.

Her throat worked. 'It's dreadfully hard to explain, but I just would rather—do it my way. I mean, thank you, I appreciate your thoughtfulness—'

'Maisie, your baby is a Dixon whether you like it or not,' he interrupted impatiently.

'What—what does that mean?' she stammered.

'We—apart from Tim,' he said drily, 'do not abandon our seed to an unknown fate.'

She fired up suddenly. 'It's not an unknown fate!'

He tipped a hand. 'Perhaps I could have phrased that a little differently. But surely, for a girl in your position, it's got to be welcome news that you'll have some back-up?'

She stared at him. Yes, it would be, in other circumstances, she had to admit. But if it meant it was going to bring her into frequent contact with this man, who was going to be hard enough to forget anyway, how much more difficult was it going to make life for her?

'I can't think straight,' she confessed. 'Look, the best thing is probably for me to go home tomorrow and just—relax and let it all settle.'

He smiled slightly. 'Good thinking actually. You can come with me.'

'Oh, I have an open-return ticket—'

'Maisie Wallis,' he said dangerously, 'don't argue with me.'

She subsided. 'Well, thank you, I guess I won't have to

change planes and sit around airports—and I'm starting to feel exhausted.'

'You're starting to look it. Go to bed,' he recommended. 'I'll make some excuse about dessert.'

But the thought of sharing a room with him suddenly hit her and he must have seen the confusion in her eyes.

He said, 'The room next door was vacated this afternoon. I've booked it.'

'But—how's that going to look? Or have you told them we're not married?'

He grimaced. 'I thought you'd be relieved. No, I haven't told them—if the task was up to you, how would you go about it?' He eyed her.

Maisie opened and closed her mouth several times but nothing came out.

'Precisely,' he murmured.

'Yes, but…'

'I've told them I need to work tonight and I don't want to disturb you. They quite understood.'

'All right,' she said after a moment.

Rafe sat by himself for a while in the Tree House and pondered the events of the day.

Such as Tim Dixon coolly admitting that, since he sometimes did get mistaken for his all-powerful cousin—it had actually happened at the wedding where he'd first laid eyes on Mairead Wallis—he might as well put it to good use as a means to attract women.

Tim Dixon, looking amused, as he recounted the irony of Maisie never having heard the name. For that matter the irony of discovering she was not nearly as sophisticated as she looked.

The *it was just one of those unfortunate things* attitude he'd displayed when he'd gone on to explain he hadn't set out to get Maisie pregnant. It had been an oversight, she'd been innocent enough to be deceived, and anyway, how many virgins fell pregnant the first time?

And finally the bitter antagonism that had intensified when Tim Dixon had gone on to explain that he hadn't meant to walk away so soon either—not that he'd ever had any plans to marry Maisie—but several creditors had chosen to make flight his only option over a jail sentence at that time, and Tonga had seemed to be the answer.

It had occurred to Rafe to remind his embittered cousin, two years his junior, of the sizeable settlement he'd received in lieu of suing for a lost cause. But he knew it was too late to change anything.

Tim *had* grown up in his shadow and, despite the generosity of Rafe's mother, Tim's own mother had never forgiven the Dixon family. Rafe hadn't realised how much of it had rubbed off on Tim until it was too late.

It had occurred to him that Tim could so easily have gone the other way—he had so much going for him. Or had there been a bad seed, just like his father, in his cousin right from the start?

If so, they were always destined to be enemies.

Then he'd thought of Maisie and that was when all sympathy for Tim Dixon had fled, and that was when he'd laid down the law in extremely hard, unpalatable terms, and they'd parted bitterer enemies than ever before.

So what was puzzling him now? Maisie's reaction, which had almost seemed to show that she sided with Tim Dixon?

Did it make sense?

Or did it mean she *was* still in love with Tim? Did that explain why she'd followed him to Tonga? Could she still be in love with Tim even if she could see no future with him now?

What would be so surprising about that, though? he thought cynically. Many women fell for charming rogues.

But was there something going on he didn't understand?

His mind ranged back to the previous evening and the pleasure she'd quite glowingly shown in his company—not to mention, he thought with some irony, how refreshing he found *her* company. But that didn't fit in with a girl who had had her heart broken by his cousin.

So, was she secretly hedging her bets?

Still trying to bind him in silken, subtle strands so she would at least have a stand-in, substitute father for her baby?

Or was *he* tilting at windmills? Looking for more reasons to scotch the desire he'd felt for a girl bearing another man's baby, not to mention his cousin Tim's?

James drove them to the airport the following morning, very early.

And he took it upon himself to act the tour guide, since Maisie's last trip had been in the dark, as he pointed many things out to her. The vanilla farm, the taro and breadfruit plantations and of course the banana and coconut trees that were everywhere.

She saw the king's residence in Neiafu and the magnificent Port of Refuge Harbour with many yachts at anchor.

They passed a few churches, one with its bell ringing as the congregation streamed in, and it made her sad to think she'd never got to hear a Tongan choir.

She said suddenly to James, 'What does *ofa atu* mean? I've heard it a couple of times. Goodbye?'

James shook his head. 'In Tongan it means I love you. Goodbye is *alu a* and the response is *nofo a.*'

That too, Maisie thought. I love you and goodbye…

All the things he pointed out helped to take her mind off a lonely, restless night filled with thoughts of Rafe then a poignant dream of them walking down the aisle together as man and wife that saw her wake up with tears on her cheeks.

Then wondering if she'd ever be so open to the influence of any other man, so alive to his looks and his aura; made to feel so fluttery in the stomach in his presence. Unable to cure herself of the conviction that to be in his arms and to be made love to by him would be like sheer heaven, and she'd always be lacking as a women if it never happened for her.

Yes, it had happened to her before and proved to be a terribly painful trap for the unwary, but the events of the day had taught her one thing. She'd been dazzled by Tim Dixon at a time when she was at a very low ebb. But she'd fallen in love with his cousin, who, apart from one kiss, had made no moves to attract her at all.

Nor could you compare the kind of man Tim Dixon had turned out to be, with Rafe Sanderson…

Yes, it had been a painful night, but one good thing it brought was that she fell asleep on the flight home and didn't wake until they landed.

Then there were three employees of Rafe's waiting to greet him, all, by the looks of it, desperate to get their hands on him with urgent business matters. One of them was his secretary, Jack Huston.

It was Jack who put her in a prepaid taxi after she'd said a brief goodbye to Rafe and he'd promised to be in touch.

Truth to tell, she was mentally and emotionally exhausted and she wasn't at all sure she mightn't burst into tears as he said goodbye, so it had been a relief to get away.

She assured herself she'd be in much better command of herself when she met him again, for the last time.

She assured herself she would have come up with some way to put Rafe Sanderson right out of her life.

He came to see her a week later.

She was prepared, she'd made coffee and she was going to serve it on the veranda, but before she did that she gave him a brief tour of the house at his request and explained what her parents had had in mind for it.

When they got to the veranda he looked out over the view, and he told her he could understand why she didn't want to leave.

She agreed that the view was certainly something but she added, as she poured the coffee, that she was quite resigned to leaving now.

Rafe studied her, the loose Fair Isle jumper she wore over loose trousers, her hair rather rigidly confined and the shadows under her eyes. He frowned suddenly. She wasn't glowing at the moment and you couldn't tell she was pregnant either—had her appetite deserted her and, if so, why?

'I'm afraid you are going to have to move but you don't have to lose this house, Maisie.'

She sat down opposite him. 'No, Rafe, I'm afraid I *can't* accept—'

'*You*,' he overrode her, 'are about to be splashed over the tabloids as my pregnant mistress who masqueraded as my *wife* in Tonga.'

She gasped and her eyes were aghast as she shot up then sank back into her chair. 'No,' she whispered. 'But—how?'

'Someone on Vava'u recognised me. They have the dates that Mr and Mrs Rafe Sanderson were staying there. They have pictures of us that link us inextricably to the place. They even have one of the staff confirming that it had given them great joy to welcome Mr and Mrs Sanderson.'

'I *knew* we should have…' She couldn't go on.

'Yes,' he eyed her grimly, 'hindsight is all very well but it's not going to help us—more particularly *you*—now.'

'How do you know this?'

'I was advised of this story doing the rounds by a friend in the media. I've pulled a few strings so it could take whoever this is a little time to find a buyer for their story but it's only a delaying tactic. Someone won't be able to resist getting their hands on it. That's not all, however.'

'What more could there be?' she cried.

His lips twisted. 'You have a short memory, Maisie. This person has done other research and come up with the rumour that we were aboard the *Mary-Lue* alone in…intimate circumstances.'

'Melissa,' she said. 'Your terrible friend, Melissa!' she accused.

He shrugged. 'We're actually related—she's a Dixon a couple of times removed. I guess that's why I put up with her.'

'Not another one—you really have an appalling family, Rafe Sanderson!'

'Some of 'em,' he agreed laconically. 'But there's only one way to counteract this.'

'What's that?' Maisie asked dazedly.

'You need to marry me.'

CHAPTER SEVEN

SHE stared at him transfixed with her lips parted and her eyes stunned. 'Marry you—oh, no!' she croaked. 'I could never—'

'Maisie,' he said impatiently then seemed to take hold, 'OK, let's take this point by point. Your job, for starters.'

'I've already accepted I'll have to leave it!'

'But have you considered the fact that you may never get another if you're splashed across the press in such a lurid manner? You might even find it hard to teach privately.'

She nearly bit her tongue as the implications hit her.

'Have you any idea what it's like to be besieged by the media?' he continued relentlessly. 'What it's like to have your whole life picked over? How do you think the retirees you play for on a Sunday would react? How do you think,' he paused, 'your parents would have reacted?'

Her eyes dilated then she blinked vigorously. 'They would have supported me, but it might never have happened to me if I hadn't been so sad and lonely.' She broke off and bit her lip.

Rafe shrugged then said more gently, 'But they're not here to support you.'

She rubbed her face agitatedly. 'All the same there must be some other way—I just can't think straight.'

He watched her. 'There are, apparently, photos taken with

a long lens through the shutters of the dining room at The Tongan of us eating together. Of you—glowing and...' He closed his eyes briefly.

'Don't go on,' Maisie whispered as she covered her burning cheeks with her palms.

'There are also a couple that appear to show you clearly wearing a wedding band and there's a claim that you were overheard telling the whale guide you wouldn't swim with the whales because you were pregnant.'

Her mind leapt back to that wonderful day with the whales, now overshadowed by the fact that someone, unbeknownst to her, had been following her every move.

'This is terrible,' she said hoarsely. 'But I could just disappear for a while, couldn't I? Yes.' She sat up straight.

'No.' He said it quite gently.

'But why not?' she protested.

'Because mud sticks, Maisie. Because,' he moved his shoulders restlessly, 'I got you into this when I should have known better.' He paused and looked irritable. 'I suppose at the back of my mind I thought we were far enough from home to be safe, and I didn't know what else to do with you. But I'm certainly not about to abandon you to the wolves.'

'But surely—I mean, it might be a nine days' wonder or...people may simply not be interested?'

His grey eyes were supremely cynical. 'If you had any idea of the lengths I have to go to—normally—to protect my privacy, especially in regard to whom I might marry...' He gestured with both hands. 'But there's something else.'

She looked at him with dread in her eyes.

'There's Tim Dixon. When this news filters through to him, I wouldn't put it past him to muddy the waters considerably by claiming the baby as his.'

Maisie went white. 'But—but,' she stammered, 'he could do that even if we were married.'

'No.' He shook his head and his grey eyes were suddenly as cold as steel. 'Tim would know better than to tangle with me over my wife. An alone-in-the-world, besieged Maisie Wallis he might even feel he has a score to settle with could be another matter.'

Maisie shivered suddenly and felt like fainting.

'Drink some coffee,' he murmured.

She did, but the only inspiration it supplied her led her into an unforeseen trap. 'But we don't want to marry each other.'

He rubbed his jaw and stared out over the harbour for a long moment then looked back into her eyes. 'Is that a hundred per cent true, Maisie? For you?'

Her colour came back although it fluctuated delicately.

'What do you mean?' she asked with her heart in her mouth.

He simply looked at her.

She got up suddenly and leant her elbows on the veranda railing with her back to him.

He waited, with his hands shoved into his pockets.

She turned at last. 'I don't know why but you make me feel safe.' She swallowed. 'You're the only person in the world who seems to have my best interests at heart. You,' she paused and smiled fleetingly, 'seem to know and understand when I'm starving and when I could fall asleep on the spot. It—it has affected me.'

She pushed some escaping curls behind her ears. 'But that's no reason to fall in love. In fact I have the best reasons in the world to—stay well away from that kind of thing. And I mean that.'

They stared at each other.

'You think you can turn these things off like a tap?' he queried then.

'I know I have to. I know I have to rely on myself now and I will,' she said with quiet decision and patted her stomach. 'Plus, I can't believe any man could want me like this, let alone a man who could have anyone he chose. I really can't.' Her eyes were suddenly dark with conviction.

'What makes you think I could have anyone I chose?'

She raised her eyebrows. 'Your wealth, the fact that you can be rather nice when you're not in dictator mode—you told me yourself women are always throwing themselves in your path.'

He smiled drily. 'I've successfully avoided marrying any of them to date.'

She frowned suddenly. 'Why? I mean you say that—I don't know, but with some…hidden meaning.'

'Perhaps I haven't been able to sort the wheat from the chaff. Perhaps no wheat has actually presented itself yet.'

'What do you mean?' Her frown grew deeper.

'I mean no one has come up with a good reason *not* to marry me yet.' He looked at her ironically. 'You're the first, Maisie. The ledger always seems to have been weighted in the wrong direction, you might say. Until now.'

She digested this incredulously. 'Are you saying—what are you saying?'

'I'm saying the fact that you don't want to marry me has,' he looked out over the harbour again with his eyes narrowed against the sunlight, 'a curious appeal.'

'But surely all the other women—surely amongst them *some* of them must have been, well, nice and…' She stopped in confusion.

Rafe Sanderson grimaced over the word *nice* then he found

himself thinking of Alicia Hindmarsh. 'Yes, very nice,' he said soberly, 'but still with that one ambition.'

'I'm—nonplussed,' she confessed.

A glint of humour lit his eyes. 'Don't worry about it,' he advised. 'We all have our strange little quirks, no doubt. Nor does it alter the fact that you really have no choice, Maisie. Unless you relish the thought of being portrayed as a girl who slept her way around the South Pacific?'

She flinched visibly. 'But they could still do that even if we married,' she pointed out.

He shook his head decisively. 'No. Don't you see? As a married couple, all the newsworthiness goes out of the story.'

Maisie covered her face with her hands then came back to sit down, and forced herself to think straight. 'But what kind of a marriage?'

He sat back. 'A marriage in name only until the baby comes. The advantages of that should be obvious. I have the means to keep you safe and secure throughout what is a vulnerable time for any girl, but for you much more so now. Then,' he paused and studied her, 'well, time will tell. We may find it suits us but, if not, a little further down the track we can discreetly dissolve it.'

'Suits us?' she echoed.

For a moment he looked amused. 'As you once remarked, it's about time I settled down since you clearly believe I have one foot in the grave.'

'I didn't say that! I didn't mean it either!'

'No, but you did say I wasn't getting any younger. Look.' He sat forward. 'We, each for our own reasons, do not appear to view love and all the trimmings through rose-coloured glasses. That doesn't mean to say we couldn't make a marriage work. But of course, only time will tell.'

Bewilderment, shock and confusion chased through her eyes. Then she experienced the strangest sensation, a little flutter within, and her lips parted, her eyes widened and she put her hands on her stomach as she felt it again.

'What?' he asked with a frown.

'It moved,' she breathed. 'It—moved. The baby.'

'First time?' he queried.

She nodded.

'Do you know what it is?'

'A girl.' Her eyes softened. 'I've just had a scan. I'm going to call her Susannah, after my mother. I've already started to call her Susie, for short. I—sometimes talk to her, just nonsense. Does she think she'll have red hair?' Her green eyes twinkled and were incredibly tender for a moment, then she sobered abruptly.

'Perhaps Susie agrees with me,' he said wryly. Then his face changed. 'And perhaps, Maisie, that's what you should think of foremost—your baby.'

An extraordinary clarity of vision suddenly came to Maisie. If she didn't marry Rafe Sanderson, what future could she offer a child? A lurid past, her reputation in tatters, always looking over her shoulder, finding it hard to get a job unless she moved elsewhere and tried to start a new life…

'I…' She took several breaths. 'You could be right. I don't seem to have much option. But it is not something I would do under any other circumstances.'

He said nothing.

'I know that sounds ungracious—'

'It sounds typically Maisie Wallis,' he drawled. 'But perhaps this will ease your conscience or your sensibilities. I feel some responsibility for you, I am after all distantly related to your baby, and I wouldn't have allowed you to do anything else.'

'You…you,' she spluttered but couldn't go on.

He stood up. 'Believe me, Maisie. But look, let's make the best of things. Surely this must lift quite a weight off your shoulders?'

Only to be replaced by another weight? she wondered. The weight of loving you when I know it can't be returned?

She licked her lips. 'Yes,' she said only, though.

CHAPTER EIGHT

Two weeks later, Maisie read about herself in the paper.

> *In a surprise statement, Rafael Sanderson, previously one of the country's most eligible bachelors as the CEO of Sanderson Minerals and the head of the Dixon pastoralist empire, announced that he had married in an entirely private family ceremony. Little is known of his wife, Mairead Sanderson née Wallis, and no details of the wedding were given.*

Above the article were two photos, one of Rafe in a dinner suit and one of Maisie, a studio portrait Rafe had organised and supplied to the paper. In it she looked very expensive, wearing a chartreuse linen designer outfit against a floral background and sporting an exquisite engagement ring, a baguette emerald surrounded by diamonds.

But Maisie also thought she looked like a startled deer about to take flight.

The speed with which Rafe had moved had almost taken Maisie's breath away.

She'd moved into a luxurious apartment two days after his

visit, an apartment leased in Jack Huston's name. She'd been relieved to be able to do so after she'd answered the phone at her home several times but the caller had hung up.

That was when it had really hit—the awful feeling that there were prying eyes out there, possibly even people following her. She found herself looking over her shoulder a lot. That was when she'd really started to feel dreadfully alone and afraid…

Then—she hadn't been sure if this was a relief or not— Rafe had had to fly to Melbourne for several days on urgent, unexpected business…and his sister, Sonia, had come to stay with Maisie…

'I have no idea how I'm supposed to feel about this,' she swept into the apartment saying, 'but I'm Sonia Sanderson, Rafe tells me he's marrying you and he needs me to look after you for a few days— Oh!' She stopped abruptly and regarded Maisie with her hands on her hips and a frown.

Sonia was dark with flashing eyes and an imperious air. She took in Maisie's stretch tartan tights and loose fleecy-lined green top, her hair gathered in a bunch of curls, her flat ballet-style shoes. 'You're not exactly what I expected,' she added.

'You don't have to stay and look after me,' Maisie said quietly. 'I can look after myself.'

'My dear,' Sonia said caustically, 'despite the fact that I'm his *older* sister, like everyone else, when Rafe says jump, I jump.'

'So I've experienced,' Maisie replied with obvious bitterness.

Several expressions chased through Sonia's eyes.

Then she said, 'Let's start again. Should we be friends? Because I get the feeling you might be in need of a friend and I'm actually rather fond of Rafe despite his infuriating ways. I believe you're pregnant and that bastard Tim Dixon is responsible?'

Maisie sat down unexpectedly and burst into tears. Sonia brought her tissues and patted her shoulder then she made a cup of tea.

When the worst of it was over and Maisie was sipping her tea gratefully, she said, 'Sorry. I've actually placed a ban on any more tears; I don't usually cry at the drop of a hat but…' She gestured a little helplessly.

'Pregnancy alone can do that to you, as I should know, having been there three times myself, but a contretemps of this nature on top of it…' Sonia shrugged. 'But you have agreed to marry Rafe, haven't you?'

'Only because I won't have a shred of reputation left to me if I don't and that's not the kind of background I want for this baby. No child deserves that.'

'So,' Sonia paused, 'does he make your skin crawl or something like that?'

Maisie blinked. 'Rafe?'

'Yes.'

'No! I mean, no, he doesn't, but,' she hesitated, 'that's no reason to get married.'

Sonia eyed her for a long moment. 'Is there anyone in your life who would strongly object to you marrying Rafe?'

'No.'

'Is there any part of your life that's going to be hard to give up?'

Maisie paused. 'I loved my job but that's definitely gone and, really, I can only blame myself for that.' She pinched her nose then blew it. 'Otherwise,' she shrugged, 'I'm only twenty-two so it's not as if anything had been cast in concrete for me. Still…' She threaded her fingers together.

Sonia said shrewdly, 'Are you afraid of falling in love with Rafe? You know, you two could find you're right for each other. If nothing else, he must be very concerned about you to do this.'

'I think,' Maisie said carefully, 'that falling in love with him would be a very foolish thing for a girl like me to do. Can you imagine your brother wanting someone carrying another man's child?'

'No.' Sonia sighed. 'Especially not Tim Dixon's. I'm sorry,' she added immediately, 'please don't take that the wrong way. I just—' she banged her palm on her forehead '—can be the most tactless person sometimes. But look, may I stay? And if you are going to marry Rafe, may I help you through it?'

Sonia had been invaluable as company and in a practical way.

Maisie had discovered, when she'd enquired who was looking after Sonia's children, that Rafe's sister was separated from her husband, although fairly amicably apparently, and their father was looking after them.

So far as practicalities went, Sonia had insisted that Maisie would need a new wardrobe and not only to accommodate her expanding waist, as she put it.

'It hasn't expanded that much yet and I think the idea is for me to be in seclusion, anyway,' Maisie protested.

'It will! And seclusion maybe but not solitary confinement!' Sonia shot back then grinned. 'Besides which, shopping is therapeutic, and if anyone can afford it, Rafe can. Anyway, summer's coming and who doesn't shop for the change of seasons?'

So Maisie had acquired a new wardrobe of specifically designed clothes to suit her condition, clothes that made her realise she was growing at last even if it wasn't visible in the right clothes.

They hadn't even had to go out to do this. Several calls from Sonia plus an astute fashion sense and, almost as if she'd waved a magic wand, a selection of clothes came to them from a variety of her favourite boutiques and department stores.

Maisie had had to marvel at the powers of wealth, then she'd had to smile when Sonia had the nerve to drive a hard bargain at the same time.

Unfortunately, *she'd* been hard put to throw herself heart and soul into this exercise because she'd found herself feeling a bit like Cinderella, and not at all sure that she wanted to be on the receiving end of such largesse from Rafe.

But when Sonia had divined this she'd pointed out that the clothes were props really and, if Maisie was going to marry Rafe and have the whole world believe it, she needed to look and feel the part.

'There's nothing worse than feeling out of place, clothes-wise,' she said stringently. 'Now for the wedding outfit. White?' she went on to query.

'No. I'm not entitled to wear white.'

'Oh, phooey, who cares about that old tradition?'

'And I wouldn't even if I were,' Maisie persisted, 'because I look dreadful in white.'

Sonia laughed. 'OK! I give up! We'll look for something else.'

The result had been a beautiful silk tapestry suit in a pale peppermint-green, so artfully designed you wouldn't have known she was pregnant.

In between putting together a wardrobe, Jack Huston had come to see Maisie several times.

She liked him. He was quiet, tall and gangly, he treated her with deference whatever his feelings on this out-of-the-blue marriage of his boss's—though did she but know it, he'd been shocked into utter, unblinking silence on hearing the news.

Then he'd got another shock when she'd made her wishes known to him when he brought up the subject of her house.

'Yes, I've been thinking,' she said. 'I—'

'Rafe doesn't want you to sell it,' he broke in.

'Rafe…' Maisie hesitated and changed tack. 'No, I won't, at the moment. But I'd like to rent it out until, and if, I decide to sell it. That way any repairs, and the rates, would be taken care of, so, well, they wouldn't be a drain on Rafe.'

A drain on Rafe Sanderson? Jack Huston thought incredulously.

'Would you be able to arrange that, Jack?' she asked anxiously.

'Yes, of course. Um—I believe there's also a boat?'

Maisie fought a private little battle with herself. 'I—I would like to sell it.'

He told her that he could arrange that for her as well, then he produced some papers. 'If you could let me have your passport and sign these I could get it changed to your married name. I could do the same for your bank accounts et cetera.'

She agreed but she drew the line at anyone but herself severing her connection with the band, or resigning her job for her.

'I think,' Jack said carefully when she voiced this opinion, 'it's important for them to know you're getting married and to whom. You could emphasise that because he is who he is, to protect you from any unwelcome publicity, it's been a behind-the-scenes matter.'

She agreed again after a long moment but that was when it dawned on her that Jack Huston knew more about her than she'd realised, perhaps all there was to know but specifically that this exercise in marrying Rafael Sanderson was designed to protect her name.

And she'd appreciated all the more his practical, deferential manner, but the deep reservations she had about marrying Rafe Sanderson hadn't gone away.

Then Rafe had come home and, without quite knowing how it started, they'd had their first row the moment they'd laid eyes on each other again, two days before the wedding…

It was about five o'clock in the afternoon and Maisie had spent most of her day trying on clothes, hats, shoes—everything, really.

When Sonia left to go and see her children she decided to have a shower, and when she came out of it she tied her hair in a bunch on top of her head with a green ribbon and put on a new outfit she'd acquired for her trousseau.

She had no idea whether it was unlucky to wear your trousseau before the wedding but the long-sleeved, loose wool top the colour of heather and gun-metal satin trousers, with an expanding waistline, seemed to suit her mood.

'Well, Maisie.' Rafe strolled into the apartment, using a key she didn't know he had, and found her in her bedroom, 'has Sonia been looking after you?'

She jumped and dropped a pile of gorgeous lingerie she'd been sorting. 'I didn't hear— How did you get—? Don't *do* that, Rafe! You don't *own* me yet.'

It wasn't what she'd planned to say, it seemed to come out of its own accord, but her heart was still banging with fright and, if she was honest, her usual reaction to Rafe Sanderson when she hadn't seen him for a while.

He raised his eyebrows. He was casually dressed in jeans

and a round-necked grey jumper she recognised. And he took in her bunch of curls and the ribbon, the droplets of moisture still sliding down her slender neck and her bare feet.

'Who said anything about owning you?' he drawled. 'And why so jumpy?'

She licked her lips—*why so jumpy*? 'You accused me of it once but *you* must have a remarkably short memory! Thanks to you I'm in hiding, I'm scared to show my face and I'm not enjoying it.'

'Thanks to me is debatable,' he shot back. 'You were the one who snuck aboard the *Mary-Lue* and nearly drowned me, which actually, whatever you might like to think, presaged all that followed.'

She opened her mouth to fire back an angry retort but he added coldly, 'You were the one to follow me to Tonga without having the sense to make sure you had accommodation.'

She paled but her eyes darkened. 'Why on earth you want to marry such an idiot is beyond me, Rafe!'

'Stop it,' he commanded through his teeth, and grasped her wrist. 'I know, and *you* know, it's the only thing to do.'

'That doesn't mean to say I have to like it. Let me go!' She tugged at her wrist but he held on fast.

'No. Not yet.' His face was set in harsh lines and his mouth was hard. 'Not until we've sorted this out. Yes, we've both made mistakes. No, I don't think you're an idiot—unless,' he said deliberately, 'you plan to make heavy weather of this all the way?'

She stared up into his eyes. 'What do you suggest? That I give in to my natural inclination and make love to you instead?'

Of course, it was anger that had made her say it, her temper taking control, and it was meant as a jibe at him along the lines of 'no doubt, as a man, you see that as the obvious solution!'

But what it did instead was expose the crux of her problem in all its raw honesty to her. Because it wasn't only anger that was causing her breasts to heave beneath the fine wool. No sooner had the words left her mouth than she became incredibly alive to all the things Rafe Sanderson did to her.

That fluttery sensation at the pit of her stomach was there. The desire to experience all the power and glory of his beautiful body on her own burned through her at the same time as, on a mental level, she wanted to be able to be relaxed and happy and in love with him.

It also exposed something new to her, an adult feeling as if she'd left Maisie Wallis way behind her. The girl who'd been more innocent and naïve than she'd ever realised. A girl who had had no idea you could be furiously angry with a man and still want him at the same time but perhaps supremely, a girl who hadn't realised that the consequences of loving one man unwisely didn't stop you from loving another…

'I'm sorry, I'm really sorry!' She rushed into speech as a tide of colour rushed into her cheeks, as a nerve fluttered wildly at the base of her throat and she felt her nipples jut against the wool of her top.

Oh, please, don't let him notice, she prayed, and added, almost tripping over her words, 'That—that was a nasty thing to s-say and I wouldn't have if you hadn't annoyed the life out of me as well as frightening the life out of me.' She broke off and bit her lip. 'That probably doesn't make sense.'

He released her abruptly and studied the more rounded lines of her figure beneath the heather top and satin trousers, then he looked into her anxious eyes. 'Yes, it does. It's the truth that often gets thrown up in the heat of the moment and I should have thought of—frightening you, anyway.'

She plaited her fingers. 'I keep looking over my shoulder,

I can't seem to help myself.' She looked around and sniffed. 'As for owning me, I can't help feeling considerably in your debt. All these…' she gestured at the clothes she was sorting '…they make me uncomfortable.'

'Maisie?'

He waited until she was finally able to bring herself to look at him, to find his expression austere and unreadable. 'Perhaps the solution is to make this a real marriage. We are two mature adults, aren't we?'

'Rafe.' She paused and sniffed again, then she sighed. 'Thank you, and I do seem to have grown up pretty fast lately. But I guess one thing that won't change about me is the conviction that it needs to be love, not lust, for me, for the next time around—if there ever is a next time around.'

'Sometimes the first can grow from the second.'

She shrugged and tried to make light of things. 'Maybe I'll always be strictly a horse-before-the-cart kind of girl from now on. But don't worry about it, I'll be fine. This rarefied sort of life is getting on my nerves, that's all. Although your sister has been marvellous.'

He looked at her drily. 'If for no other reason than the fact that my sister has given me to understand she'll personally strangle me if you come to any harm at my hands, we will find a way to make this work, Maisie.'

Maisie blinked. 'Sonia said that?'

'More or less. And Sonia, mad, is not to be trifled with.'

Maisie had to laugh, and finally the situation was defused.

He stayed to have a drink with her, and he told her about the plans he'd made for after their wedding—a week in the country.

'Not—not Karoo?' she queried warily.

'No, another station, with not a Dixon in sight.'

'That's a rel…' Maisie stopped awkwardly.

He raised an eyebrow. 'A relief? I realise you're not a fan of the Dixons in general but we aren't all—'

'No, I meant, it's a relief there'll be no family to have to put on a charade for.'

'Ah.' Something flickered at the backs of his eyes. 'No, there won't. There will be staff but they have their own quarters. I thought you might find it interesting. I happen to love it and sometimes I'd give my right arm to spend more time there.'

'How will we get there?'

'By helicopter.'

Maisie found herself watching him out of new eyes for a moment. As if she was glimpsing another fascinating facet of Rafe Sanderson.

'However,' he said then, 'after that we'll come back here to Brisbane and we'll get down to where you'd like to be based.'

Sonia came back at that point. She poured herself a drink and updated Rafe on the arrangements she'd made for the wedding day.

'The marriage celebrant will arrive at your apartment at eleven. We'll be there then, so will Jack, and I'll arrange to get all Maisie's stuff sent over earlier. Any objections?'

Rafe raised his glass to her. 'Beloved, I don't know what I'd do without you.'

He left not long after that and he and Sonia had a short private conversation as he was leaving. Maisie didn't ask what it was about, and Sonia didn't offer to tell her.

Truth to tell, Maisie had more on her mind than what Sonia and Rafe had been discussing.

Had she given her feelings away to Rafe? Was that why he'd suggested a real marriage? But why would he even be thinking along those lines unless—as he'd intimated when he'd asked her, no, *told* her he was going to marry her—it was a marriage he needed to make rather than wanted to make?

So how would she feel about that? A marriage, not in name only but a marriage of convenience, all the same, for them both?

Terrible…

The next morning all, so far as Maisie believed anyway, was revealed about Sonia and Rafe's private conversation—a day at the beach accompanied by Sonia's children.

Maisie had already met the twelve-year-old Marcus, ten-year-old Hilary and nine-year-old Cecelia, and liked them, although she'd decided a little wryly they were the only people in the world who were excited about this forthcoming wedding.

But a day at the beach was an inspired idea on a clear, sunny morning. Although it was a day at the beach done in the style only the very rich could afford.

Sonia had booked two interconnecting rooms at a lovely resort hotel right on the beach at the Gold Coast and just across the road from the exclusive shopping of the Marina Mirage Centre, for the day. And it worked wonderfully well. They swam and romped on the beach in the morning, they had lunch around the pool then they had two cool, stylish rooms to retire to, to shower and change and relax for a while before they went shopping.

Maisie did take the precaution of wearing a concealing hat and dark glasses, and Sonia did the same, but it was a fun expedition with no unpleasant surprises.

Then they had an exquisite afternoon tea at the Palazzo Versace, next door to the Marina Mirage, before driving home, all pleasantly tired.

'Was that Rafe's idea?' Maisie enquired after they'd dropped the kids off.

Sonia nodded. 'He was worried about you. He reckoned you needed a bit of a break. Are you going to be all right tomorrow?' she asked directly.

Maisie drew a deep breath. 'Yes.'

And that conviction stayed with her, helped by a good night's sleep, through most of the next day…

But Sonia had another surprise up her sleeve. She somehow turned a wedding between two people marrying for all the wrong reasons into a festive affair.

After the short ceremony presided over by the marriage celebrant, Marcus, Hilary and Cecilia, all beautifully dressed, showered them excitedly with rose petals and confetti.

Not only that, but there were also flowers everywhere, champagne on ice and a wedding lunch laid out—even a cake.

So it was a lively lunch for them all. Jack was a surprisingly entertaining guest and proposed a brief but rather sweet and funny toast to the bride and groom.

Then Sonia gathered her offspring and took her leave along with Jack.

She kissed Maisie warmly then she kissed her brother, but her expression directed at him as she stepped into the lift somehow said very much in an older-sister manner—*it's up to you now; don't let me down!*

Both Rafe and Maisie found themselves smiling ruefully as the lift doors closed silently.

'She is a character,' he murmured.

'Yes, but she's been lovely to me. Is there any hope she and her husband can get back together?'

Rafe sighed and shrugged as he pulled off his tie. 'I keep

trying to promote it, but really, only Sonia can do it. She…
Put it this way, I don't think Liam, her husband, feels he's ever
broken through, or will be able to, to the real Sonia.'

Maisie blinked. 'Not even three children later?'

'Not even three children later,' he repeated. 'There are
reasons why she likes to keep a part of herself to herself but
we won't go into that now. OK. We have half an hour to get
changed and get to the airport. Think you can do it?'

'Yes, but—' Maisie looked around a bit dazedly '—we
can't leave all this.'

'The same team who put it together will dismantle it. Off
you go.'

She bit her lip and went. Obviously, there was going to be
more than the obvious to get used to in her new life.

She shed her green silk suit, her pale stockings and changed
into loose long trousers and a shirt. Her clothes had been
brought from the leased apartment and her bag for the trip out
west was packed and ready. Then she stared at the suit hanging
up in the closet.

Rafe hadn't commented on her appearance but his eyes had
softened for a moment as they'd rested on her, and he'd
handed her a beautiful posy of white violets.

That had been a tricky moment, she reflected. It had
brought a lump to her throat.

She looked around and reregistered the fact that she'd been
given what was obviously the master bedroom in his apartment on the river, with great views, a huge bed and a décor
of taupe on raspberry.

It was a beautiful room but why had he moved out? She'd
have been perfectly happy with a guest bedroom… Why did
this room, this whole apartment make her feel uneasy?

'Ready, Maisie?' Rafe called through the door.

She took a deep breath. 'Coming!' And she positioned the broad-brimmed khaki felt hat, a hat Sonia had insisted was *de rigueur* for a sheep-farmer's wife, on her head at a jaunty angle.

CHAPTER NINE

SHE should have expected it but had not—that Rafe would pilot his own helicopter.

She'd never flown in a helicopter before but she found the experience fascinating and she was even more fascinated to discover that he had actually flown round Australia by helicopter.

'This one?'

'Yep! I made some modifications to it for the trip. I put in some long-range fuel tanks, somewhat to the detriment of seating accommodation. It's basically only a two-seater bird now but she has plenty of range.'

And he told her a bit about his trip, which made her green with envy.

Then they intercepted a mayday call on the VHF radio.

They were west of the Darling Downs, where the country was drier, although there was still some feed, dusty, criss-crossed by stock trails and sparsely populated and they were heading into the setting sun.

She had her own headphones, principally so she and Rafe could converse above the noise, but she was also tuned into the three-way conversation that ensued.

It was an accident at a cattle-muster camp with a man requiring urgent medical attention or evacuation to the nearest hospital.

The Flying Doctor responded immediately from their base in Charleville while Maisie stared down at the desolate terrain they were flying over, her heart in her mouth as the man from the muster camp reported the injured man's condition.

'Poor bloke,' Rafe murmured. 'Sounds like spinal injuries, which may mean he shouldn't be moved without a doctor present.'

Then Maisie heard the man reporting the accident say tinnily, '…won't get a fixed-wing aircraft in, country's too rough, we need a chopper…'

That was when Rafe transmitted to report his position, not that far as the crow flew from the muster camp.

'Hotel Zulu 459,' the Flying Doctor base came back, 'we don't feel the patient should be moved without medical supervision but would you be able to render any assistance in the meantime?'

'Hotel Zulu 459 back to Base,' Rafe responded, 'I do have a comprehensive medical kit on board and some first-aid training. Muster Camp, Muster Camp, this is 459, can you give me a more accurate idea of your location?'

'Muster Camp back to 459,' came the tinny voice, 'I've got a GPS here in the ute; I'll get the reading off it. Hang on, mate.'

'Thank heavens for that,' Rafe murmured, twisting his microphone away from his mouth for a moment. 'I'm sorry about this, Maisie, it may not be pleasant but—'

'Oh, don't worry about me,' she said immediately.

He gave her a quick pat on the knee and twisted his mike back into place.

As the latitude and longitude co-ordinates came through, she watched him punch them into his GPS, set a target then read off the distance and time to target. 'OK, Base,' he said into the mike, 'we're about twenty minutes away. Let us know what you want us to do.'

'Stand by 459,' Base responded. 'I have a doctor coming on air to talk to you.'

It turned out, as Rafe discussed the situation with the doctor, that he had sufficient training and the right medication on board to be able to stabilise the patient until a bigger State Emergency Services helicopter with a doctor on board could be flown to the site to supervise the patient's removal, hopefully within a couple of hours at the most.

'There!' Maisie breathed and pointed to a pall of dust rising into the air above the rocky, uneven ground below away to her left. 'It looks as if they've got some cattle in a pen of some kind and—and I can see a ute, two of them, some horses and a makeshift kind of camp.'

'That's it. Looks like they've spread a sheet on the ground where it's most level.' He spoke into his mike again. 'Muster Camp from 459, make sure those cattle can't break out, mate, I need to know that before we come in, in case we spook them.'

He said it quite casually but Maisie closed her eyes in fright.

'459, it's a permanent yard—they can't go nowhere. See the sheet we laid out?'

'Affirmative. OK, I'm coming in.'

'You can open your eyes now, Maisie. We're safe and sound on the ground and there are no stampeding cattle to deal with.'

Her lashes flew up and she heaved a sigh of relief, to see Rafe looking at her with a little glint of devilry in his eyes before he turned his attention back to shutting the helicopter down.

'Sorry,' she said. 'It's not that I don't have great faith in you—'

'It's OK. You've been terrific. Many a girl I know would have had the screaming heebie-jeebies. Right. Let's see what I can do.'

Three hours later Rafe was still in charge of the patient because the SES helicopter had developed engine problems and had had to return to its base.

Maisie had sat around the camp fire, the muster crew had gone out of their way to make her as comfortable possible, and they'd cooked dinner on the fire and produced plenty of strong coffee.

But it was a tense time. Even the cattle in the yard were restless under a paper-thin wedge of new moon and bright starlight as they shuffled and lowed. And the dust caked everything.

It had been a freak accident. The ringer involved had been thrown from his horse when a snake had wriggled across its path, right next to the camp. Fortunately that meant they hadn't had to move him—they'd moved part of the camp instead so there was cover to protect him from the sun earlier and now the dew.

But it was obvious from his grey, sweat-streaked face that he was in considerable pain despite Rafe's ministrations and the splint he'd put on his broken arm. And it was plain that he couldn't move his legs, which was terrifying him.

'Al,' Rafe said abruptly to the camp foreman, when they got the news the SES helicopter had had to turn back, 'could you rig up some kind of shelter for my wife and maybe lend her a swag?'

'Sure thing, Rafe.'

'I'm fine,' Maisie protested. 'You don't have to worry about me.'

'Little lady, you do what your husband suggests,' Al recommended. 'We'd all be happier if you didn't have to go through much more.'

She hesitated but there wasn't anything she could do.

So they set up makeshift shelter for her and built a fire in front of it to keep her warm. Then they laid out two swags and gave her two blankets.

'But what about you?' she asked.

'None of us is going to sleep anytime soon,' Al responded. 'Anyway, we're tough. You get a bit of rest,' he added and patted her shoulder in a fatherly way.

Rafe came over to her then with her bag and a mohair blanket from the helicopter.

'I'd just add some clothes,' he recommended. 'It's going to get really cold. And if you need to go to the loo, I'm happy to ride shotgun.'

'Oh, thanks!' she said with real gratitude.

She discovered the bed they'd made for her on the ground was bearable, and she dozed for a couple of hours.

Then she heard a helicopter overhead and the terrain outside her shelter was bathed in the harsh blue light of its searchlights as it reconnoitred. She heard shouts to move the kerosene lamps to indicate a slightly different landing pad, then the ground shook as the helicopter settled and a minor dust storm flew past her shelter.

She couldn't hear much of what was said because the cattle had become thoroughly stirred up again but some time later the helicopter lifted off, there was a renewed bovine commotion, more dust—and Rafe came to join her.

He added a log to the fire and dropped down beside her makeshift bed.

'Move over, Mrs Sanderson, I'm coming in and I'm bloody freezing!'

Maisie moved over instinctively and he crawled in beside her.

'Mmm…' he murmured as he wrapped his arms around her. 'As warm as toast.'

'How is he?'

'They think it could be a trapped nerve in the spine. If so, that's good news. Are you comfortable?'

'Yes. How about you?'

'Yes. Go to sleep.' He lifted a hand and stroked her hair for a while.

She couldn't help herself. She couldn't keep her eyes open and she snuggled up to him and fell asleep with her head on his shoulder.

It took Rafe Sanderson a bit longer to fall asleep as he battled several emotions.

If he put aside Tim Dixon's baby, the girl in his arms felt almost as if she belonged there. He certainly felt a sense of responsibility towards her. He couldn't help admiring her pluck and her honesty…

He grimaced to himself in the firelight as he recalled his first, harsh reaction to her incredible story—that she was on the make somehow, that she expected him to be moved enough to hand over some cash to her for just those reasons. Well, he'd done far more—he'd given her the protection of his name.

Of course, although it appeared not to have struck Maisie, his own good name could do with a bit of protection against impregnating a naïve girl and flaunting her as his wife then, apparently, discarding her. And the further sleaze that could be added to the mix to do with her being passed between him and his cousin.

But what of the future? She'd admitted to feeling safe with him but had it gone any further? Or, he thought drily, were some of her reactions, reactions that sometimes prompted him to think so, still part of a policy of hedging her bets?

If so that meant she'd rather cleverly orchestrated her opposition to his proposal—she'd thought fast and on her feet.

Unless—had she always somehow divined that to make him chase her would have the curious appeal he'd actually confessed to her?

But did he really believe any of that of Maisie Wallis, feeling so soft now and lovely in his arms with her breath sweet on his neck and her lashes lying like dark fronds on her perfect skin? Hell, he thought suddenly, why am I putting myself through this?

Because you had no option, he reminded himself, other than freezing out there on the hard ground, or sitting upright in the chopper. Not to mention causing, no doubt, comment.

But what would be so bad about turning this into a real marriage, he wondered. The kind of suitable marriage he was beginning to think was going to be the solution for him.

Because it was becoming increasingly obvious to him that, for reasons known only to him—and Sonia—a *fall madly and wildly in love* marriage might not be on the cards for him.

I'll tell you why it mightn't work, he responded to himself: Tim Dixon's baby. You might be able to cope with it and all the scenarios it raises in your mind in a marriage of convenience with no real love lost, but otherwise, who's to say it wouldn't become a real thorn in your side?

What does "otherwise" mean? he asked himself incredulously. That you could, against all probability, find yourself falling in love with Maisie Wallis?

The thought, and its implications, shook him. Another came hard on its heels: if she was hedging her bets but a secret part of her could never forget Tim, they could have the makings of a private little hell between them.

So was she right? he wondered with self-directed irony.

Not only right but also honest when she'd said she was going to have to turn certain things off like a tap—to wit, feeling safe in his arms, although, he thought with further irony, she hadn't been able to get that quite right yet.

Mind you, circumstances hadn't helped on either occasion, he acknowledged.

But—he clenched his jaw and eased himself a little away from her—she wasn't the only one going to have to nip certain things in the bud; so was he…

At least until he'd sorted whether this marriage could prove to be workable rather than a minefield.

When Maisie woke, dawn was lightening the sky and Rafe was fast asleep beside her. She sat up cautiously but he didn't move.

The fire had died but there were sounds coming from beyond the shelter. She heard horses whickering, the creak of leather and the clink of metal shoes on rock. She heard subdued voices and a dog bark.

Al had explained to her last night that they would have to move the mob of cattle on to the next drinking hole as early as possible and she guessed that operation was getting underway, which meant that they'd also be striking camp.

She turned reluctantly to wake Rafe, to find that he'd opened his eyes, and she found herself drawn into a long exchange of glances with him that somehow took in the night they'd spent together in such close proximity.

Colour mounted in her cheeks as she remembered cuddling up to him this time and how wonderful it had felt.

But what she saw in his eyes, as she couldn't hide what was in hers, affected her deeply. It was as if a shutter had come down so they were unreadable and steely grey.

'Tea's up!' a voice called. 'Tea's up!' And Al appeared

carrying a blackened billycan with a rag wound round its handle, and two tin mugs. 'Sorry to wake you guys but—'

'That's OK!' Rafe sat up then got up and stretched. 'Thanks, mate. We'll get going pronto.'

And Maisie, after Al had departed, desperate for something to say to ease her discomfort, grumbled, 'I don't know why, but when there's absolutely nothing between us we keep getting caught in bed by an audience!'

Whether it struck the right note or not, she didn't know.

Rafe smiled briefly, a rather ironic little smile, then a moment of genuine mirth overtook them, followed by a touch of concern.

'You—you look like a North American Indian,' she said incredulously.

'And if you could see yourself!' He held down a hand to help her up, his eyes alight with laughter, then he ran his tongue over his teeth. 'I can even taste the blasted dust.' He paused as she put her hand to her back and grimaced. 'What's wrong?'

'Nothing! Well, just a twinge. Probably even two swags on the ground take a bit of getting used to.'

'Hmm… OK, have your tea—at least it's hot and wet— and we'll get going.'

It wasn't until they'd farewelled the muster camp and the helicopter rose like a bird above it, that he told her of his change of plan. They were going home.

She protested that she was fine. He said he'd like to get it checked out all the same, and there was absolutely nothing she could do.

But she was unable to stop herself wondering if this was somehow bound up with that steely, shuttered look that had come to him and had made *her* feel so—what?

Rejected?

Could he be using it to get out of being in her close company for the next week?

I knew I should never have married him, she thought. I knew I was beyond the pale…

'Maisie, how would you like to live?'

They were alone in the apartment on the river; it was the same evening. His doctor had checked her out meticulously in an evening house call, something she'd thought was unheard of these days. He'd pronounced that the baby appeared to be fine and she'd probably just been a bit stiff from a night of sleeping virtually on the ground.

'Well, at least we know,' Rafe said, and added his question.

'How would I like to live?' she echoed. 'I'm not sure what you mean.'

They'd had dinner, sent up from the restaurant on the ground floor, causing her to marvel how easy life was for the rich. She'd also been drawn like a magnet to his magnificent sound system and asked if she could play some music. He'd told her she didn't have to ask so she chose a CD of classical piano pieces.

'We have a couple of options: this apartment, or I have a house at Raby Bay.'

'Oh, look, whatever is best for you! I—don't mind.'

He came to sit down on the settee set corner-wise opposite her.

There was a single lamp lit on the end table between the settees and its soft golden glow bathed them before receding into the coral shadows of the lounge.

Through the terrace doors, the lights of Brisbane twinkled against a midnight-blue backdrop although it was only about eight o'clock.

Maisie had changed into her heather outfit and, although her feet were bare, she was sitting rather primly upright with her hands in her lap, as if she didn't feel particularly at home, which she didn't.

Rafe also had bare feet but he looked much more relaxed in cargo shorts and a white knit shirt. In fact he had his feet propped on the coffee-table and one arm stretched along the back of the settee.

'No,' he said. 'I can base myself anywhere within reason. You're another matter. You're going to need to feel at home, perhaps a bit involved with that home, and comfortable. This,' he gestured towards the view, 'may be a fabulous setting but I don't know if it's going to do that for you.'

Maisie took a startled breath. 'How did you know?'

He raised an eyebrow at her.

'That, well, a little while ago I was looking around and wondering what on earth I was going to do with myself here for the next five months.'

He shrugged. 'I'm not entirely insensitive.'

'I didn't say you were.' She shook her head.

He watched her curls settle. 'So would you like to look at Raby Bay? There's a garden; it's right on the water with a jetty, so I could move the *Mary-Lue* there for—any free time we have. The other advantage of it is that Sonia only lives a couple of blocks away.'

'Yes, please. It's also closer to my stamping ground, the bay-side suburbs of Wynnum, Cleveland and so on, so—I would feel more at home, I guess.'

'All right, we'll do it tomorrow. Tell me something else. Were you serious about wanting to get your Master's Degree in music?'

She sat forward eagerly. 'Yes!'

'How would you go about it?'

'I'd have to enroll as an external student, I'd have to get a tutor, I'd have to practise,' she looked comical, 'day and night. And it could take years.'

'I gather you'd also need a piano?'

'No, my piano is fine. I'd just have to get it tuned after it's moved. Am I dreaming or is this all possible?' she asked.

He studied the excited little glint in her eyes as he thought, all? It didn't take much to please Maisie Wallis.

'It's all possible. Now, Miss Mozart, it's been a long day, you need to get to bed. Incidentally, I checked with the Flying Doctor. They operated on the ringer at Charleville Hospital and he's regained movement in his legs.'

'That's wonderful!' Maisie brightened, and discovered for some strange reason that the news made her feel better about being dismissed to bed like a child, despite the fact that she'd started to feel weary. 'OK. Goodnight! And thanks!' she called over her shoulder.

'Goodnight,' he murmured, and watched her all the way out of the lounge.

Then he rubbed his jaw, set his teeth for a moment but finally congratulated himself on his executive abilities even when it came to his home life…

Maisie fell in love with the two-storey Raby Bay house as soon as she saw the stone walls and blue shutters.

It stood on two blocks in the prestigious canal-side estate—the canals opened on to Moreton Bay. From the street side it was enclosed by a high stone wall and it was surrounded by trees, some carrying a light cloak of new spring green.

The path to the front door was covered by a thatched pergola.

Inside, on the ground floor, the walls were the same uneven stone as outside, the floors were tiled and the water views—views she loved—were seen through arched, wood-framed, floor-to-ceiling windows.

And everywhere in the living rooms lovely wood was blended with the stone and other natural elements like terracotta and pottery; there were paintings and exquisite pieces of furniture in an uncluttered, spacious interior.

The patio that led off the main lounge was tiled with grey slate and had a grapevine trained to shelter one end from the sun.

Leading off the kitchen was a small walled courtyard Rafe called the "orangery" because of the lemon, lime and orange trees in tubs. There was also a number of herbs growing in a variety of unusual containers like a pot-bellied little black stove.

Upstairs was different, more conventional. The walls were lined, plastered and painted, the floors covered with thick wall-to-wall carpet, but lovely and luxurious all the same.

Maisie came down the curved staircase with its wrought-iron bowed banister and stood in the middle of the lounge.

Rafe followed her and came to stand beside her. 'Well?'

She turned to him and tilted her chin imperiously. 'I'll take it,' she murmured grandly, then burst out laughing. 'Oh, Rafe, it's wonderful! Why don't you live here?'

He grimaced. 'It's—somehow it's not the kind of place you enjoy rattling around in on your own.'

'Someone does, though, by the looks of it. It's all spotless and the garden's well cared-for.'

'A cleaner comes in once a week, ditto a gardener.'

'So whose idea was it?'

'My mother's.' For a moment she thought she saw a shadow cross his eyes, but it was gone before she could be sure. 'It was her favourite home. Right. How soon do you think you'd like to move in, ma'am?'

'As soon as possible, Mr Sanderson. As soon as possible.'

It took a week, but before they moved to Raby Bay Maisie had to endure a rather taxing event, a meet-the-family soirée organized by Sonia but a strategy agreed upon by Rafe as well.

He said, with a wry twist of his lips, 'Of course they're all wildly curious, I can't keep you under wraps from them for ever so we might as well get it over and done with.'

'But a soirée! And how many?' Maisie asked a little faintly. 'Do they know I'm pregnant?' She put her hands to her head in a gesture that was extremely expressive of dazed disbelief or as if she was contemplating being thrust into a den of lions.

Rafe grinned. 'They're not going to eat you. Yes, some of them can be a bit daunting but just be yourself. And, since you still don't look pregnant at times, particularly to anyone who doesn't know you, we may just let that bit of news filter through in due course.'

She coloured a little.

If he noticed it, he gave no sign as he went on, 'Sonia does that kind of thing really well. In fact she's a genius at handling parties so they go without a hitch.'

'She might need to be,' Maisie murmured. 'Do you really think we need to do this?' she asked with a frown in her eyes. 'Because we aren't—we don't…' She stopped awkwardly.

'We don't know each other in the biblical sense?' he supplied a little drily. 'I really think,' he paused, 'all we need to show is that we're friends.'

'There,' Sonia said just before her soirée was about to get underway. 'You look lovely.'

They were in Sonia's bedroom at Raby Bay. Maisie stared at her image in the long mirror and conceded to herself that she was happy with the way she looked, although how she felt was another matter.

The outfit she and Sonia had chosen was black voile over a taffeta lining; a sleeveless, hip-length blouson top and a slim skirt. The silky voile was sheer from the tops of her breasts over her shoulders, and black really highlighted her glowing, smooth skin, plus the voile over a taffeta lining felt floaty and looked wonderfully dressy.

Her legs were bare and her high, slender-heeled strappy sandals were black patent with rhinestones studded on them.

She and Sonia had spent a couple of hours in Sonia's favourite beauty salon so they were perfumed and beautifully groomed. Once again Maisie's hair was teased out and her red curls shone. Her make-up was less than full-stage but accentuated her eyes, and her lips were painted a shimmering, deep-tawny colour.

Her fingernails, although short, as they had to be for a pianist, were beautifully manicured and painted to match her lips. So were her toes.

'You probably wouldn't know,' she said as she turned to look at herself side-on, 'that I'm pregnant.'

'No, you wouldn't,' Rafe said, coming into the room. 'You look…you both look wonderful.'

Sonia laughed. 'If I'm any judge, your wife is going to steal the show, Rafe. OK.' She glanced at her watch. 'Heavens above, it's a quarter to four—only fifteen minutes! Excuse me, you two.' And she bustled out.

Maisie hesitated. 'You don't look too bad yourself,' she said, and winced inwardly because she thought he looked sensational in a light grey suit with a navy shirt and tie.

He shrugged. 'Thanks. I've got something to add to your outfit.' And he pulled a leather box from his pocket. He opened it to reveal a diamond pendant on a silver strand circular necklet.

Maisie gasped as the stone lay in his palm, reflecting fire from its facets. 'Who—whose is that?' she stammered.

'It was my mother's but—'

'I can't wear that—if that's what you had in mind,' she amended.

'It is what I had in mind,' he said with some irony, 'because to those in the know, it will really set the seal on our marriage—and that's what we want, don't we, Maisie?'

'Well, yes, but it must be worth a fortune and—no, no, I couldn't accept your mother's jewellery.'

'It's not precisely in the nature of a gift,' he said. 'You're right, it is worth a fortune, so after this…outing it will go back to the bank.'

'Thank heavens!' she breathed. 'But I still wouldn't feel right about wearing it!'

'Maisie,' he eyed her with a mixture of exasperation and something she couldn't identify, 'trust me and just do it!'

She eyed him back with her chin tilted.

'Please,' he added with a sudden smile lurking at the backs of his eyes.

It undid her, that smile. It actually turned her to jelly inside, and she nodded, barely perceptibly.

'Turn round,' he said.

She did, slowly.

He looped the circlet around her neck and did up the catch. His fingers were warm on her skin and she closed her eyes briefly then opened them to squint down at the stone lying just below the round neckline of her dress.

Then she looked up and their gazes caught and held in the

mirror and it shook her to think that they looked—what was the word?—so fit for each other, she in her beautiful outfit and perfectly groomed, he, so tall and masculine…

And she found herself holding her breath for a moment as he looked down at her, and his hands moved at his sides and she thought, she really thought he was going to put his arms around her.

It didn't happen, and when he looked into her eyes again, his were as shuttered as she'd seen them once before, at the muster camp.

She let out a long, uneven breath and he turned away.

'Ready?'

'Yes.'

But she was far from ready for anything, until, as they went downstairs together, she remembered her last practical music exam for her bachelor's degree.

She'd been so nervous she'd been convinced she would fail dismally, but at the last minute before she sat down at the piano she'd thought to herself, you can do this. Just put yourself in a bubble and don't let anything else intrude, not moderators, not the fact that it's a strange piano, nothing but you and your music.

And that's what I need to do now, she thought as she reached the bottom of the staircase at her husband's side. Take Rafe's advice and put myself in a bubble where I can only be myself despite ubiquitous Dixons, despite being pregnant to a man who is not my husband, despite Rafe…

Sonia had a conservatory overlooking the water and there were about twenty people gathered amidst the potted plants and the cane and rattan furniture. It was an elegant, charming area and there was a piano at one end.

There was a white-coated steward serving champagne and a pretty girl dispensing canapés.

About an hour into the soirée Rafe Sanderson watched his wife from across the room, and marvelled a little.

He and Sonia had stayed close throughout the introductions to three of his aunts and their husbands, assorted cousins and their partners and several nieces and nephews.

Then Sonia had moved away to work her entertaining magic, that knack she had of getting her guests to relax so that soon the conservatory had come alive with animated conversation and laughter. And Maisie had got separated from him but she'd handled it with the poise of—of course, he thought to himself—Mairead Wallis.

'But what brought you two together?' he heard one of his aunts, a dragon-lady according to the younger members of the clan, ask.

'Well, I guess you could say it was sailing,' Maisie responded then smiled enchantingly. 'A bit like Crown Prince Frederik of Denmark and Mary Donaldson, except that our Ship Inn was the *Mary-Lue*.'

His dragon aunt Nancy, he saw, looked gratified, and he had to award Maisie ten out of ten for an inspired response that not only had elements of truth in it, but also elevated this unknown girl he'd married to suitable heights.

On the other hand, she does think fast on her feet, he reflected, and found the thought niggled him.

'So what are you?' he heard his cousin Amelia, pure Dixon from her sculpted fair hair and grey eyes down to the pointed toes of her handmade Jimmy Choo shoes, enquire. 'Do you have a career?'

'Yes,' he heard Maisie reply, 'music. I taught it but now I'm studying for my Master's Degree.'

'Do you perform?'

'Yes, well, I have.'

'A chamber orchestra, a quartet?'

'No, much livelier than that.' Maisie bestowed a sparkling green look on Amelia. 'Jazz, rhythm and blues, disco—that kind of thing, in a band.'

Amelia raised her eyebrows and Rafe moved forward to stop what he knew was going to be inevitable, but he was too late.

'Do give us a tune, then,' Amelia said, her well-bred tones just a little sceptical.

He saw Sonia zooming in from the other side of the conservatory.

But Maisie bestowed another charming, bewitching smile on his cousin, and said, 'With pleasure! Although I'll make it short.'

'You don't have to,' he murmured, reaching her side.

'Oh, I don't mind. It's about the only credential I have,' she added for his ears only, and slipped her arm through his. 'Lead me to it.'

Ten minutes later she'd wowed the gathering, and left some egg on the face of his cousin Amelia, with a lively, sparkling medley excerpt of well-known tunes, from a stunning "Rhapsody in Blue" through to the latest pop song that was at the top of the charts. They begged her not to stop.

'Yes, yes, I must!' And she got up and closed the piano. 'Thank you for being such a lovely audience,' she added warmly.

And as she came back to his side, he knew that Maisie Wallis had endeared herself to his family.

Snippets of conversation reinforced this.

'A genuine *ingénue*…'

'Rather refreshing, wouldn't you say…?'

'So lovely and natural…'

'Well, I didn't know what to think but I'm converted…'

'The only thing I don't understand is why all the secrecy…?'

He saw Maisie catch that comment, and in her only un-guarded moment her eyes flew to his and he thought he saw something curiously stricken in them.

'That wasn't so bad, was it?'

They'd driven back to the apartment and Maisie was sitting on a settee, massaging her feet, having kicked off her shoes.

'No, I suppose not,' she said quietly.

He slung his jacket and tie over a chair and unbuttoned his shirt at the neck.

'You say that as if you have reservations.'

She looked up at him. 'Yes, I do. It was basically dishon-est and,' she sighed, 'I—I don't feel too good about myself.'

'You certainly put on a sparkling performance.'

She grimaced. 'A bit of that goes directly to having red hair. It seems to sort of…put you on your mettle, and I guess I thought, well, I can only be myself. But of course, that was only the tip of the iceberg.'

She reached behind her and unclasped the diamond neck-lace. 'Thank you.' She held it out to him. Then she suddenly looked directly into his eyes. 'You say that as if you have res-ervations.'

'Say what?'

'That I put on a sparkling performance.'

He gazed down at her, still so elegant in her lovely black dress even with bare feet, but with shadows in her green eyes, then he shrugged. 'Perhaps I only meant that it was Mairead, not Maisie, who took over tonight.'

Maisie examined the uneasy thread that lay between them she was coming to know well and she said, before she stopped to think, 'You don't like Mairead, do you?'

'I didn't say that,' he denied, 'but I do find her a bit—I don't know, but it may have something to do with—it was Maisie I met first.'

Or because Mairead leads straight back to Tim Dixon? she found herself wondering, and shivered suddenly.

'What's wrong?'

'Nothing,' she murmured but wondered for a moment if she could explain that it wasn't only redheadedness that went into Mairead. Yes, she might be able to extend that confident aura to suit the situation at times but basically it came from her music.

Once she'd discovered that "bubble" in her practical exam, it had provided what probably all performers, be they ever so different at other times, drew on. That almost spiritual affinity with their music.

But would he believe that?

'Maisie?'

She shrugged. 'I really am one and the same person. A bit battered now, shop-soiled, some people might even say, but if,' she gestured, palms out, 'all this hadn't happened I would have lived with my mistakes and made the best of things.'

He frowned. 'What are you saying, Maisie?'

'I guess, that people are going to have to take me or leave me.'

'As in me?' he queried abruptly.

She stood up and picked up her shoes. 'No, Rafe, not you. You've done enough, you've literally picked up the pieces—I don't expect any more from you.'

'Maisie,' he said harshly, then paused because the only way he knew to defuse things between them was to take her in his arms, to kiss her and cradle her to him and tell her—what?

That Mairead both attracted him and disturbed him? Because Mairead was more enigmatic than Maisie at the same time as she was…stunning? But beneath that vivacious, on-her-mettle personality, what really lay in her mind?

Come to that, did he still feel bound up in silken strands?

Talking of silk, he mused as he studied the pearly glow of her skin beneath the unlined voile of the top of her bodice, he contemplated drawing her dress down her body so none of that smooth, lovely skin was veiled and hidden from him.

He wondered what expressions would chase through her green eyes as he did so.

On the other hand, he reminded himself, he felt real affection for Maisie, perhaps too much to put her through the mill of his indecision—and the other reason he was the way he was.

But, and it was a bit like slamming into a wall, yes, there were still moments when he could forget she was pregnant and by whom but shortly that wasn't going to be possible. Soon, every time he looked at her he was going to be reminded of his charming, feckless cousin…

Not only that, but he was also going to be asking himself if she still loved Tim. He'd never forgotten her remark in the Tree House that had seemed to indicate she was looking for excuses for Tim.

He shut his teeth hard. 'Maisie, let's just get through your pregnancy, let's take one thing at a time, in other words. We've done what had to be done and perhaps both of us, but you particularly, need a break.'

She swung her shoes in her hand. 'Of course. Goodnight, Rafe.'

He watched her go and was almost unbearably tempted to stop her, to throw all caution to the wind, but he didn't.

He made a savage little sound in his throat and crossed the room to pour himself a nightcap. He swirled the brandy and gazed into its amber depths.

It couldn't work, he told himself. Maybe if it had been anyone but Tim, who will no doubt think it was a nice revenge to have foisted his baby on me, maybe…

But it wasn't only Tim Dixon who held him back, it was the fact that he well knew how destructive a love-hate relationship could be. After all, he'd lived through one.

Maisie fell asleep with relative ease.

It was as if she'd made a statement about herself she'd needed to make. It was as if she'd finally closed the door on her feelings for Rafe Sanderson.

Three days later they were both installed in the house although the apartment was to be maintained.

Two months later, despite her ongoing love affair with the house, Maisie dropped her head into her hands as she sat at her piano, and tears trickled through her fingers.

The dog curled up on the floor beside her sat up and put a paw on her lap.

She fondled its silky head and pulled a hanky from her pocket to blow her nose.

The dog, a present from Rafe, was a six-month-old border collie that she'd christened Wesley, Wes for short. And it was a living example of everything her husband had done for her to make her life pleasant and bearable over the last months, but there was so much more.

He'd installed a live-in housekeeper—there was a small service flat over the garage—so she would never be alone. Grace Hardy, in her forties and a spinster with a childcare background, was unobtrusive but they'd become friends when they'd discovered two common interests—Grace loved to cook and she belonged to a choral society.

Maisie had also become friends with the gardener, who'd been delighted when his role of simply a maintenance gardener had been expanded, and together they'd planned and planted a summer garden.

The *Mary-Lue* was now tied up to the jetty on the canal and they'd taken her out for some glorious sails, although never alone, always with Sonia and the children.

Sonia—and Maisie believed it was not because she was jumping to her brother's tune but out of genuine affection—had become a good friend.

They shopped together, they lunched together at Cleveland's trendy pavement cafés, they went to the movies and concerts. They popped in and out of each other's houses when the whim took them and Maisie was giving Cecelia piano lessons. She often babysat the kids for Sonia, not that they were babies, but she loved it when the stone house with its blue shutters rang with young voices and laughter.

She'd met Liam, Sonia's husband, and liked him as well as pondering what had separated Sonia from him. Rafe had never gone on to explain further.

Thanks, she had no doubt, to the influence Rafe exercised over his family, even on this occasion his cousin Amelia and his aunt Nancy, the news of her pregnancy was well-received.

She often thought to ask him if they knew who the baby's father was but, since no one ever mentioned Tim Dixon to her, she gathered that Rafe had kept his own counsel on the subject, so she decided she would do the same. To be honest, it gave her a headache even to think of how that bit of news could be explained.

The Tonga story and its potentially disastrous consequences for Maisie Wallis had never surfaced. As Rafe had predicted, once their marriage had been announced, there was little newsworthiness in it.

In fact, she'd often thought that Maisie Wallis had disappeared, been swallowed up in her new life. She'd even contributed to it—for some reason, she'd never visited Manly, she'd never gone back to see the *Amelie* or her parents' house. She'd left it all in Jack's hands.

She had a music tutor and she'd embarked on her Master's Degree with enthusiasm.

But now, sitting in front of her piano at seven and a half months pregnant, there was not an ounce of enthusiasm in her for anyone or anything, least of all herself, and she knew precisely why.

It all came under one heading—Rafe. And the fact that that it had been a vain assumption that she'd closed the door on how she felt about him.

He was kind, he took an interest in her interests but she sensed a brick wall between them below the surface and, as she'd once feared, it was hurting her almost unbearably.

He was rarely home, but even when he was in Brisbane he didn't always sleep at the house, he used the apartment, and that added another torment for Maisie. Did he have a mistress, and if so, could she blame him?

He certainly wasn't going to want her now that she was heavy, swollen and slow. Who would?

And when she couldn't control her imagination, she had a mental cast of potential lovers he might chose from, from statuesque brunettes through to creamy, glorious blondes.

If you added to all that blotches of brown pigment on your skin, heartburn that interfered with your sleep and the conviction that this pregnancy was never going to end, it wasn't easy to feel chipper.

Not even the nursery she and Sonia had decorated, the shopping they'd done for the baby, not even the thought of her child, the lifeline she'd clung to for so long, was helping her because she'd started to question her suitability as a mother.

Who wouldn't, she thought, when you couldn't give your baby a father because you'd ignored all the conventions and good sense you'd been brought up with and allowed yourself to be swept off your feet and, if that wasn't bad enough, when you'd fallen in love with another man not long afterwards?

Was it any wonder Rafe Sanderson viewed her as foolish, if not worse? She was… Although she still hoped and prayed that she hadn't given away what she felt for him.

She'd also come to the growing realisation that being a single parent was extremely lonely on a mental plane, even leading the cushioned, want-for-nothing life she was living.

Yes, she could talk to Sonia about anything to do with babies and birth but nothing could replace the link she was missing, the spiritual link she needed with the other half of her baby's creator. Not that Tim Dixon could have ever given her that, she knew; no one could now—that was what made it so lonely.

'Yoo-hoo! Anyone home?'

Maisie scrubbed her face urgently as Wes stood up and barked once then wagged his tail.

It was Sonia, but despite her bright greeting she looked unwell, even unusually haggard, as she walked into the den that had been converted into a music room.

'What's wrong?' Maisie asked.

'Nothing! I'm as right as rain.' She patted Wes then she added rigidly, 'What I need is a good, stiff drink.'

Maisie opened her mouth, closed it and said, 'Sit down, I'll get you one.'

And she did so as fast as she could.

'Now,' she handed Sonia a crystal tumbler with a generous tot of brandy in it, 'what's wrong?'

Sonia accepted the glass, sipped and choked. 'Liam's asked for a divorce,' she said with tears rolling down her cheeks. 'And it's all my fault.'

'Why?' Maisie queried gently.

'Because I'm a fool,' Sonia said tragically. 'It's taken this to make me realise that I drove him away because I'm really cynical about letting anyone get too close to me. I thought I could have Liam yet keep him at arm's length. I was even convinced,' she laughed hollowly, 'that he'd come back after he asked for a separation, it just needed a little time.'

She breathed raggedly then continued, 'I thought I should always be in command of myself but that led to wanting to be in command of him too on top of,' she paused and pressed her fingers to her temples, 'a natural tendency to bossiness anyway,' she said with bleak honesty.

Maisie sat down on a cushioned footstool in front of her sister-in-law. 'Oh, Sonia, I'm so sorry. But—why? What made you like that?'

It was Sonia's turn to scrub her face. 'When you grow up in a war zone you tend *not* to allow yourself to feel anything too deeply.'

Maisie's eyes widened. 'A war zone? I don't understand.'

'My parents had a love-hate relationship that was,' Sonia shook her head, 'deeply disturbing, sometimes terrifying as a child living through it. I suppose I took my mother's side instinctively and subconsciously decided never to put myself in a position as painful as hers.'

She pleated her skirt and shrugged. 'But, you know, you grow up and you think you've put it all behind you—until one day you wake up and realise it caused you to build a fence around your emotions that you can't seem to break through. Or couldn't.' New tears welled. 'And now it's too late.'

Maisie put her arms around her.

And she sat deep in thought after Sonia had left.

Were daughters more vulnerable in that kind of situation? In other words, how had his parents' turbulent relationship affected Rafe? Was he just as cynical in his own way as Sonia?

Did that explain why a man who had so much to offer, you would have thought, had no time for a wife and family?

What had he said to her once? Something about neither of them, for reasons of their own, viewing love and all the trimmings through rose-coloured glasses…

'The evidence,' she murmured aloud, 'seems to be piling up against him ever falling in love with you, Maisie, if that's what's in your secret heart—and of course it is! Not that this makes any difference. Tim Dixon was always going to effectively scotch that possibility but why does this news disturb me so much?'

It was a question she couldn't answer, she could only acknowledge that it lay heavily on her mind.

It was to be a day of bad news.

Rafe came home earlier than he usually did on a weekday, and found her in the kitchen making dinner.

'What are you doing?' he asked as he pulled off his tie and flicked open the top button of his shirt.

'I am concocting,' she said brightly—she'd perfected a bright, breezy manner with him, 'a chicken casserole with Marsala, mushrooms, parsley, capsicum, shallots and that's about it.' She waved a hand over the series of bowls containing her colourful ingredients. 'Oh, and bacon.'

'Where's Grace?' He opened the fridge and took out a can of beer and a bottle of unsweetened apple juice, which happened to be Maisie's favourite drink of the moment.

'She's gone to a choir rehearsal. Anyway, I felt like cooking.'

He poured the beer into a long glass and the apple juice into a shorter one. 'Come out onto the patio, I need to talk to you.'

'That sounds serious. Can't we talk while I cook?'

He shook his head and after a moment she untied her apron and turned off the pan she'd been about to sauté the mushrooms, shallots, capsicum and bacon in.

And she followed him out onto the patio where he studied the *Mary-Lue* bobbing a bit on the end of the jetty as a boat wake rocked it.

Then he turned to her. 'Tim—has died, Maisie.' And he watched her reaction like a hawk.

CHAPTER TEN

SHE went white and had to sit down heavily. *'Died?'* she repeated hoarsely. 'How?'

'In a diving accident in Vava'u. He actually saved someone's life at the expense of his own.' He told her some of the details. 'He…I'm bringing his body home; I'll leave this evening in about an hour, so I should be home tomorrow morning. We'll only stay to refuel.'

She stared at him, still clearly in shock. Then she placed her hands on her stomach as if trying to shield her baby from the news, and Rafe Sanderson made his own deductions.

'I'm sorry,' he said very quietly.

'I—I don't know what to say.'

'You don't have to say anything. I have my own regrets about Tim. You were right, it wasn't easy for him growing up in my shadow and with an embittered mother in the background. I should have—taken that into account a lot earlier than I did. That's why I don't want him to make his last journey home alone.'

Tears were sliding unnoticed down Maisie's cheeks and once again Wes, who followed her everywhere, put his paw on her lap.

'But,' Rafe went on when she tried to speak but couldn't,

'what time will Grace get home? I don't want to leave you alone...I know, I'll ask Sonia—'

'No.' Maisie found her voice. 'She's—got her own problems. And Grace should be back shortly.'

'What problems?' He frowned.

'Liam wants a divorce and it's hit her for six.'

He swore softly. 'I'll give her a call. Maisie—will you be all right?'

'Yes. Really! I'm fine, so don't worry about me.' She looked away from him. 'It—it was just—a shock.'

'Naturally.' He paused. 'Come and help me pack.'

'I... Would you mind if I just sat here alone for a little while, Rafe?'

For some reason he frowned but then he shrugged. 'Sure. But think of this, Maisie. He died a hero and that's how Tim was. He could be very bad but when he was good he was good.' And he went inside.

Leaving Maisie to ask herself exactly what she did feel over this news. Shocked, of course. Moved to tears for her baby, who would never have the opportunity to know her father and might have wanted to one day, whatever he was like, and who was to say he mightn't have reformed his ways? Perhaps.

Maybe even moved to tears for someone who had been so full of life but whose life had gone horribly wrong...

But bereft?

No, she realised, because her closure with Tim Dixon had come in a little palm-thatch hut perched on a rock groyne in Tonga.

That was when she'd realised she was well and truly out of love with him—if she'd ever been in love with him in the first place.

So, some sadness, yes. But not the dreadful pain of losing someone beloved that she knew so well from losing her parents...

'Don't do anything I wouldn't,' Rafe said.

His bag stood in the middle of the lounge; he'd changed into khaki trousers, a check shirt and a corduroy jacket.

'I won't,' Maisie promised.

He studied her for a moment. The long, pretty Paisley cotton dress she wore, her blue sandals that she probably couldn't see over her bump now, the curiously steady green eyes—was she still in shock? he wondered.

'Feeling better?' he queried. 'By the way, Sonia is coming over, after dinner.'

'Oh, you didn't have to! Anyway,' she paused as she heard a car, 'there's Grace now.'

'She wanted to. Tim was also her cousin.'

'Thanks,' Maisie said huskily. 'Look, I'll be fine. Don't worry about me. And I think what you're doing is very—appropriate.'

He lifted a hand, hesitated, then dropped it to his side, and said goodbye.

What had he been going to do? Maisie wondered as she watched him stride out with his bag.

Did he think she hadn't noticed that he avoided all physical contact with her?

She put her hands to her face briefly then made a bright effort to greet Grace when all she wanted was to be alone.

But Grace had a request. Her mother wasn't feeling well, so would it be OK if she went over to spend a few hours with her?

Yes, fine! Maisie agreed and came to another decision.

She rang Sonia and told her she needed an early night so not to worry about coming round. Then she said abruptly to Sonia, 'Go and see Liam and tell him.'

She heard Sonia's indrawn breath, then, 'No, it's too late. It can't change anything now and—'

'Yes, it can. Maybe not for him but, now you've come to understand about the emotional fences, it's no good still hiding behind them. It may be painful but it's got to be liberating for you at least to be honest with him.'

'But that might make him feel sorry for me!'

'It might but don't accept it. Life—life isn't always easy but if being honest with yourself, really honest, means you have to be honest with Liam, in the long run *that* will help you.'

There was a stunned silence down the line then Sonia said, 'Maisie? Are you all right? You sound—is it Tim?'

'No. Of course it's sad, but—no. How do I sound anyway?' she asked ruefully.

Sonia hesitated. 'Rather wise and clear-sighted. Rather—' she hesitated again then chuckled briefly '—decisive. And I suppose you've got Grace but—I still don't know if I can do it.'

Maisie didn't enlighten her about Grace. 'Yes, you can,' she said. 'Sonia, can I tell you something? I will anyway. I admire you tremendously, you've been a wonderful friend and thank you so much, but trust me, I know you can do this and I know you should. Do it now.'

'So I did,' Sonia Sanderson said distraughtly to her brother the next day, 'with the most amazing consequences, but I had no idea she was actually saying goodbye to me! None at all, otherwise I would have gone straight over. And then—and then Grace went to see her mother and she was sure Maisie had gone to bed when she got home quite late until it struck her that Wes was restless, you know how he gets when Maisie is not around, so she went to check and—and she was gone. So were some of her clothes and the baby's.'

Rafe swore. They were driving home from the airport, where Sonia had met him, and they'd stood together side by side on the tarmac, with heads bowed, as Tim Dixon's coffin was unloaded from the plane and given into the undertaker's care.

'Did she leave a note?'

'No, nothing. Oh, Rafe, what are we going to do?'

'Get her back,' he said briefly.

'How?'

'At nearly eight months pregnant, she's not going to go far.' A muscle flickered in his jaw.

He swung the car into the Raby Bay driveway and Grace came running out of the house.

'Maisie's in hospital! She had a minor traffic accident but they took her to hospital because she was pregnant and insisted on keeping her in overnight. Then she went into labour this morning, thankfully still in hospital, so they decided to ignore her request that nobody should be notified, and they tracked down the car. Oh, I feel so terrible!'

'And if only I hadn't been so wrapped up in my own affairs,' Sonia cried.

'Enough,' Rafe growled. 'Which hospital, Grace?'

She told him.

'Coming?' He glanced at Sonia.

'Of course!'

Susannah Wallis made a surprisingly determined entry into the world, despite being six weeks early. She was rushed to the neonatal unit and a humidicrib.

Maisie got through it somehow but the pain-shot shadows she drifted in and out of were made all the worse by the concern that she'd brought this on herself. If she hadn't been driving with an overburdened mind and a mist of tears in her eyes, she might have been able to avoid the accident.

Rafe and Sonia Sanderson arrived an hour after the event.

They were told that Maisie was fine but sedated because she seemed to be a bit more traumatised than was normal. They were told that the baby was expected to overcome the potential complications of her premature birth.

'Did the accident bring it on?' Rafe asked.

The doctor scratched his head. 'That's hard to say. Maisie did present symptoms of concussion, that's why we kept her in, but no other injuries. I would have expected her, if the shock of the accident had caused it, to go into labour sooner, but there's really no set formula for it. And, for instance, some premature births are simply spontaneous, in that, at least half of them have no known cause.'

'Can stress be a factor?'

Sonia found herself holding her breath as Rafe asked this.

'It can, yes. But before she embarks on any more pregnancies, Maisie should be checked for any uterine malfunctions that can, for example, cause premature birth, just to be on the safe side.'

'Rafe,' Sonia said, as they waited for Maisie to come round, 'don't blame yourself. You did everything you could for her.'

'Except give her back to Tim,' he murmured.

Sonia's eyes widened. 'Is that why she ran away? But would she have taken Tim back? From what you told me, he didn't want her.'

'Does that make you stop wanting someone?' Rafe shoved a hand through his hair. 'And something traumatised her into going. It had to be the news of Tim.'

He stared at Maisie looking so pale but with a livid bruise

down one side of her face, and curiously frail in the hospital bed, as if all her sparkling vitality had been quenched.

She was hooked up to a drip and she had a name tag on one wrist; and he sighed heavily.

Maisie grew properly lucid that afternoon.

She'd known Rafe was there beside her bed for some time but the sedation had kept claiming her back into its soothing arms. Then it began to release her and at last her eyes were clear, she moved and pushed herself up a little.

'Maisie,' Rafe said, and took her hand, 'they think the baby's going to be fine, although they'll keep her in the premmie ward for a while.'

Her fingers clutched his as a rush of relief hit her.

Then she frowned. 'Are you sure? You're not just saying it?'

He shook his head. 'She's also got your hair. Well,' he smiled, 'what there is of it is definitely gingery.'

'Oh! I tried to tell her that if she had any say in the matter she'd be much better off as a blonde.' Her eyes, so green against the unusual pallor of her skin, were humorous but she sobered rapidly.

'Rafe—Rafe,' she said and licked her dry lips, 'you must be angry—I was going to post a letter to you…' She found she couldn't go on.

'Maisie, I was much more concerned than anything else. But this is not the time for recriminations or explanations or decisions—except one.' His eyes were steady and she suddenly realised he was paler than normal.

'You need,' he went on, 'to recoup your strength and Susie is going to need all your care and attention for the next few months. Will you come back to Raby Bay, at least for the time being?'

She drew a deep breath—and nodded. 'Thank you,' she whispered.

'You—' But he stopped as Sonia tiptoed in, bearing two lidded paper cups of coffee.

And Sonia, after she'd assured herself Maisie was as well as could be in the circumstances, flung her arms around her sister-in-law and hugged her almost fiercely.

'You were right. I went to see Liam and I told him all about me and how his news had acted as some sort of catalyst that made me really understand. But I said I was only telling him so I could come to terms with myself so he wasn't to worry or feel guilty or sorry for me. Do you know what he said?'

Maisie shook her head somewhat dazedly.

'That he'd only asked for a divorce because the separation was killing him but his pride wouldn't allow him to say so!'

Maisie was given a sleeping pill that night despite the fact that she was exhausted. She was also sore and feeling strung-up and desperately anxious to be able to see her baby—they'd told her she could do that tomorrow—and supremely conscious of the irony of her situation.

Because her "clear-sighted wisdom" had worked for Sonia but not for her. Indeed, it had been born from her decision to leave Rafe, and explain, in all honesty, why she had reached it.

So she'd written a letter she'd planned to leave in the house for him. At the last minute she'd taken it with her and decided to post it to him just in case anyone else found it.

It was still sitting in her bag.

And she was now committed to going back to him for the time being anyway. But could she handle him knowing the truth for however long that "time being" might take?

She didn't think so…

CHAPTER ELEVEN

THREE months later, Maisie nursed Susannah in her arms and sang softly to her on the patio at Raby Bay.

Wes was curled up at her feet and Susie was watching the pattern of light and shade the grapevine was creating. Then her lashes sank and she fell asleep.

Maisie rocked her a little longer, kissed her softly then she put her into her pram and adjusted the net. Susie didn't stir.

'There you go, Wes,' Maisie murmured to the dog, 'one contented baby! We're getting pretty good at this!'

She got up and wandered to the edge of the patio where she stood looking out over the water but as if she was looking far, far away to a distant horizon…

That was when Rafe, who'd watched the little tableau of a girl and her baby unseen from inside, came to a decision.

Susie was thriving now and the ordeal of the neonatal clinic was well and truly behind them. Some complications had arisen but Maisie had been marvellous in the way she'd coped, refusing ever to lose hope.

Of course, it had been an anxious time when the baby had first come home, but once again Maisie had proved equal to the task.

And now she was a calm, relaxed mother and you could never doubt she adored her baby.

She was also looking well and slim again but there was something elusive about her; just occasionally, the smallest hint of a haunting sadness.

He had no doubt what it was, just as he had no doubt the time had come to release her. But how?

In stages, he thought, that's obviously going to be the best way.

'I took a bit of a liberty with your house,' Rafe said that evening.

Maisie glanced at him across the polished surface of the dinner table. They were eating Grace's superb rack of lamb studded with rosemary tips and basted with a blend of olive oil and sun-dried tomatoes. There were side dishes of cauliflower *au gratin* and snow peas.

It was just over seven months since they'd first met and summer had slid into autumn.

Maisie had a new hairstyle, a shorter, elegant bob but still curly. She wore a sage-green waistcoat over a long-sleeved ivory blouse and black velvet trousers.

'You did?'

He nodded. 'Remember you told me about the plans your father had to renovate it? Well, I went ahead and got it done.'

She blinked at him. 'So—all the time I thought it was rented out and not being a financial burden on you the opposite was happening?'

He lifted his shoulders. 'It's been a drop in the ocean.'

She frowned suddenly. 'What about the *Amelie*? I've just realised Jack never came back to me, so I suppose it's still for sale?' She looked a question at him.

He shook his head.

'What does that mean?'

'It never went onto the market but it's in good shape.'

Maisie discovered she had difficulty with her voice. 'Why?'

'I got the impression it meant a lot to you. By the way, I'm off in a few days on a business trip for about a month.'

Maisie blinked again at this apparent *non sequitur*.

'All business?' she queried, and paused to ponder that his business lifestyle certainly wouldn't fit in with a proper married life. She articulated the thought. 'That seems rather a long time.' She put her knife and fork down and took a sip of water.

'All business, all the same.'

'Poor you,' she murmured and fingered the edge of her linen place mat before she took up her knife and fork again.

No sign of regret or even much interest, he reflected, but had he expected any? No, but that had to make it all the easier.

'When I come back,' he went on, 'I'll be moving into the apartment.'

She froze as she suddenly made the connection with her house and boat. 'Does—does that mean you're throwing me out of here?' She closed her eyes immediately in frustration— what a thing to say!

'No. I think we should stay married for a year at least, not only for Susie's sake but also the comment it might cause otherwise. If you're happy here that's fine, and you should stay as long as you like.' He gestured. 'I just wanted you to know that somewhere you seemed to love is ready and available.'

Maisie sought desperately for composure. 'Won't it cause comment—me living here, you living elsewhere?'

'Not nearly the comment a divorce after only a few months would. Anyway,' he shrugged, 'I often spend the night there when I'm flat out rather than driving here.'

It was true.

'I suppose you'd like to be able to get on with your life? I mean, that's quite natural, I'm not saying you shouldn't or anything like that,' she hastened to assure him, but, as the full implications of what this meant struck her, she pushed her half-full plate away suddenly.

Of course, there might be one special area of his life he wanted to get on with; women. Perhaps he'd already done so while she'd been so caught up with Susie so as not to even wonder lately?

'The same,' he paused and watched her for a long moment, 'could be said for you, no doubt.'

Maisie blinked several times, as if it was a completely new concept she'd been presented with.

'I…' She stopped and cleared her throat. Then she propped her elbows on the table and rested her chin on her hands. 'You know, I've been living from day to day with Susie, so it hadn't really occurred to me.'

He finished his meal and placed his napkin on the table. 'Well, there's no urgency about it.'

She opened her mouth to say 'So time has told you that being married to me doesn't suit you, Rafe?' but changed her mind because she really didn't need to be hit on the head with it, did she?

'Thank you,' she said quietly instead. 'I— Oh, there's Susie. I'm trying out a new routine in the hope that she might just start to sleep through the night.' She looked rueful.

He smiled briefly. 'Just one thing, Maisie.' He waited until he got her full attention. 'Don't disappear on me.'

Discomfort caused her cheeks to warm slightly but then she looked at him steadfastly.

And he had to acknowledge to himself that her brush with life in the raw had added maturity and character to her so that now there was a third persona, or perhaps only one now. A blending of Maisie and Mairead that was—well, he thought, he wouldn't go into that.

'No, I won't, I promise,' she said. 'Will you excuse me? She's really starting to sound desperate.'

The next two days were dreadful for Maisie.

She was forced to admit that she'd been living in another bubble for the last three months, cushioned, insulated, from her feelings for Rafe and the pain they brought her.

But that bubble had well and truly burst with this news and she was back on the rack. Even Susie sensed her agony and became fractious and weepy. And a new screw had been added to the rack—the thought of him with a mistress…

I've got to do it, Maisie thought desperately after a sleepless night walking the floor with Susie. I've got to somehow make him see I can't go on like this. I need to confront my demons, I need to get *out now*. No long-drawn-out disengagement, I couldn't stand it, and I don't care what the rest of the world thinks.

To make matters worse, although at least Rafe had been spared that long, interrupted night because he'd stayed in the apartment, she was running out of time. He was due to go overseas the day after next which meant she only had one night left to talk to him.

As it happened, she didn't even get that. She had a purely routine doctor's appointment early in the afternoon the next day and when she got home there was a message from Rafe on the answering machine saying that something had come up and he'd had to advance his travel plans, so he wouldn't be seeing her before he left. He'd added that if she had any problems to get in touch with Jack. His last words were, 'Take care of you two, Maisie Wallis.'

She was galvanised into a flood of emotion as the machine clicked off. A thoroughly old-fashioned and wifely burst of temper for one. Something was *always* coming up and the man could never be a suitable husband or father because he was a machine! An emotion that conveniently ignored how it had worked in her favour in the past, how it had taken the burden of his presence off her…

But that was immediately replaced by a sense of panic. She couldn't live the next month in the agony of indecision she was going through. She couldn't go away, she'd given her word!

Perhaps he hasn't left yet, she thought suddenly, and was galvanised into action rather than emotion this time.

She flew into the kitchen to find Grace and begged her to look after Susie for a couple of hours.

Grace, a great fan of the baby and with plenty of experience to call on anyway, was only too happy to oblige. She even advised Maisie to take her time. 'I'll make her a bottle if things get desperate. Off you go!'

Maisie flew, speed-dialling on her mobile phone at the same time.

But Rafe's number, as often happened, was on the answering service. She cut the call without leaving a message and called Jack Huston.

'Jack—has he left yet? Sorry, it's Maisie here.'

'No, I think he's still at the apartment, Maisie. Is something wrong?'

'No.' She swallowed. 'No! Just something I forgot to mention to him, Jack. I tried his mobile but it's on answer. I— It's not that important.' She hoped she sounded convincing.

'Try the apartment landline,' Jack advised.

'Thanks, I will!' She rang off and did just that. The line was engaged.

She ground her teeth in frustration then realised it meant he must still be there. She jumped into her car and set out for the city without much thought for speed limits.

She tried the number again while she was stopped at a traffic light but it was still engaged. Then she concentrated on her driving and pulled into the building forecourt with a screech of tyres.

The manager came out and she begged him to park her car for her. As she jumped out in a flurry of legs and red curls bobbing, he told her she'd just missed Rafe.

'On his way to the airport,' he added, 'and in a hurry by the look of it. You might catch him, Mrs Sanderson, but,' he raised an eyebrow, 'you know that Ferrari.'

Maisie felt herself collapse internally like a pricked balloon. 'Oh. Oh,' she whispered and closed her eyes. She knew that under normal circumstances she wouldn't catch him; she knew that even if, on the slenderest chance, she did, it would not be the time or place to explain herself.

'Well,' she opened her eyes to see the manager looking at her a little strangely, 'I will go up for a while.' She couldn't think what else to do.

'Fine. I'll put your car down in the garage. You OK?'

With an enormous effort, Maisie turned on a full-voltage smile. 'I am. I really am.'

Once upstairs in the penthouse, she sat down on the coral settee and looked around dazedly.

Then she took her mobile phone from her bag, stared at it then put it on the coffee-table as it suddenly occurred to her, from nowhere, that it was the same bag she'd taken when she'd left Raby Bay the night before Susie was born. And the letter she'd written to Rafe was still tucked into the zipped pocket, forgotten until now.

She pulled it out and read it, and for some reason it brought on a bout of painful weeping.

When the tears finally subsided, she pushed it back into her bag and she went to wash her face. She passed Rafe's study on the way and something prompted her to linger in the doorway then wander in.

The desk was tidy but his personality was printed everywhere, the high-flying businessman who controlled two empires, upon whom many jobs depended.

The man who didn't take those responsibilities lightly.

The man who had taken responsibility not only for her but also his cousin's baby.

The man for her?

She picked up a business magazine from a side-table because his face was on the cover—and shook her head.

She stared at the picture. It was all there, everything that did so much to her, despite the formality of his suit and the background of the Sanderson Minerals boardroom. From his thick hair, his grey eyes and an unsmiling, eyes-slightly-narrowed expression.

It was like having an arrow plunged into her heart, and she felt tears threatening again as she held the magazine to her breast for a moment. Then she started to put it back on the table, but the file that had been underneath it caught her eye because it bore her name.

'MAISIE'S HOUSE', she read.

She put the magazine aside and opened the file to find all the details of the renovations that had been done. There was also a marina berthing bill for the *Amelie* and three keys she recognized—the RQ gate key, the boat's engine key and its door key. They looked like the originals, so Jack must have had copies made, she guessed.

She stared at them mesmerised then took a deep, yearning breath. She would like nothing more than to be on board the boat, not going anywhere, of course, but sitting there, thinking…

She picked up the keys and slipped them into her pocket. She tidied the file and put the magazine back on top.

There was little activity on finger H at the marina. It was a windy weekday afternoon and there were even whitecaps in the harbour.

But the seagulls were active and the air was salt-laden as Maisie sat on the stern of the *Amelie*, shivering and with her hair blowing in the wind but not noticing as she thought long and hard.

Did she need to explain anything to Rafe? What would it achieve other than placing a burden on him?

Sonia's excuse, she thought and flinched, but this was different…

This was a solution—her return to her former life—he'd proposed himself, anyway, and all she needed to do was accept it, although she'd work her way towards it as soon as she could.

It spelt out, so there could be no misunderstanding, Rafe's intentions for her.

She shivered—she'd left Raby Bay in slim navy trousers and a light ivory jumper and hadn't even thought to take a jacket.

The *Amelie* was in great condition—she'd checked it all out, and she had no doubt the house would be the same, yet it depressed her terribly. Rafe Sanderson never did anything in half-measures, not even the way he made you fall in love with him, not even the way he parted from you.

She stood up abruptly and locked the boat. She climbed

down onto the jetty and started to walk away but turned to look back. The berth beside the *Amelie* was empty, so there was a clear stretch of water between her and it, and as she leant against a concrete pier pole she was partially obscured.

She sighed. There was nothing for it but to spend at least the next month at Raby Bay until Rafe came home—and that made her think of Susie, so she reached into her bag for her phone to give Grace a call. It wasn't there. She froze then clearly remembered leaving it on the coffee-table in the apartment.

'Damn,' she whispered and whirled round to run up the finger towards the gate, only to bump into a man coming in the opposite direction—Rafe, looking impossibly tall and immeasurably dangerous in the moments she had before the impact caused her to topple off the finger into the water.

He did everything he could to save her but it was no use, then he dived in after her.

'I—can—s-swim,' she tried to say as she came up spluttering and he surfaced next to her.

He took her in a lifesaver's grip. 'Have you ever tried climbing out of a marina berth? It's an invitation to get scratched to pieces on barnacles. So just shut up and do as I tell you!'

A few minutes later they were standing on the back of the *Amelie*, having used its ladder to pull themselves out of the water, and history was repeating itself as Maisie tried to catch her breath and push her streaming hair out of her eyes.

'You idiot!' he stormed at her, ignoring his soaked condition entirely. 'You also promised you wouldn't do this!'

'D-do what?' she stammered. 'It was an accident, maybe I wasn't looking where I was going but—'

To her amazement, he took her dripping figure in his arms and held her so close, she could feel his heart beating heavily.

'Not that! I mean taking flight so no one knows where you are but they do know you're upset about something.' He held her away as water streamed down his face, and continued savagely, 'Remember the last time it happened and the consequences?'

Her throat worked. 'That was entirely different. I was—I *was* running away, I'm not—'

'I know you were,' he overrode her. 'I know you got a terrible shock because you can never forget Tim Dixon, and the way he died probably brought back the best of him for you. I know I should never have left you.'

She stared up at him. His hair was plastered to his head, there were droplets on his eyelashes, but nothing hid the grimness in his eyes.

'You—you believe that?' she asked with her eyes wide and shocked.

'Of course. What else is there to believe? But while I know I have to let you go, it's going to be on my terms, Maisie, so no more frights.'

Her voice sounded strange to her as she said, 'You got a fright?'

'*Yes*. Grace, when she stopped to think about it, thought there was something a bit odd about you. Jack was convinced you were distressed about something—he virtually pulled me off the plane. You weren't answering your phone.'

She closed her eyes. 'How did you find me?' she whispered.

'I couldn't think of anywhere else to look but the house and your boat, since we were talking about them only a couple of days ago, so I took a chance. What set you off this time?' he queried harshly.

'Rafe,' her mind was whirling but it swooped on one of the things he'd said that didn't make sense, 'what did you mean when you said you knew you had to let me go?'

'Maisie…' For the first time it was no longer the hard, angry man in charge, as the lines and angles of his face settled into lines of weariness.

And he released her suddenly. 'Someone once wished this on me so it could be poetic justice, but you, of all people, should know what it's like to want someone you can't have.'

She froze. 'But—but you can't! I mean—what about your cousin, what about the kind of person that made *me*, what about—?'

He smiled drily. 'In the end, none of that mattered. Only you mattered. What kind of a person did it make you?' He shook his head. 'I suspect there was wonderful material to work with anyway but it fired you into solid gold for me. Your spirit, your endurance through what life threw at you, that spark of vitality that I only ever once saw quenched in you…'

He paused then went on with an effort. 'I was watching you the other day while you were on the patio with Susie. And it struck me that if anyone had told me a girl and her baby meant more to me than anything in the world, that she was the difference between darkness and light for me, I wouldn't have believed them. But it happened.

'And it happened,' he went on, 'with a girl I'd barely ever laid a hand on.'

Maisie swayed a little where she stood. 'But you still believed I was in love with Tim?'

'Who wouldn't?' he said tiredly. 'When the news of his death came as such a shock it sent you into early labour.'

'No.' She shook her head so droplets flew. 'It could have been the accident or—it could have happened anyway.'

'Stress can—'

'Perhaps,' she interrupted, 'but I'm the only one who knows what was really stressing me out.'

He searched her eyes with a frown in his. 'What do you mean?'

'I'm the only one who knows that I said goodbye to Tim Dixon in a little hut in Tonga because I was no longer in love with him, because I never had been. Yes, it came as a shock, his death, and it was sad.' She tipped a hand. 'Sad for Susie, sad because it was an untimely death, but devastating? No, not for me.'

'So what…?' His words hung on the air.

'It was *you* I was stressed about. I—it hit me that day that I just couldn't go on any longer, living with you, loving you but knowing there was no hope.' Her throat worked.

'But,' he paused, 'that night in the Tree House, you seemed to be looking for excuses for Tim. I've never forgotten that and what it could mean.'

Her mind flew back and she saw the candles again, their wine glasses, and heard the murmur of the sea on the beach. 'I was, but only because whether I liked it or not he's always going to be part of Susie so I wanted some mitigating circumstances for him. Something so as not to view him with utter contempt for her sake, that's all.'

His face didn't change. 'When?'

She hesitated. 'When?'

'Did you fall in love with me?'

She closed her eyes. 'When it was the last thing in the world that should have happened to me—almost from the beginning.' Her lashes lifted. 'When I loved nothing better than to be with you, when I felt safe, yes, but so much more, yet all the time I kept saying to myself—this *can't* be happening to me, but not only that, he could *never* want me.'

'Oh, Maisie,' he breathed.

But she went on, 'And that same day, the day Tim died, was the day Sonia told me all about why she was the way she was, because of your parents' marriage, and it seemed to explain why you could be cynical about love and all the trimmings. It just—it was too much on top of the misery I was already going through.' Tears beaded her lashes.

'Maisie,' this time he reached for her but only took her hand, 'yes, I was cynical. That's why I was starting to suspect only an arranged marriage was going to work for me. My parents put themselves through hell, and Sonia and I followed.' He sighed. 'But you gave no sign of distress until I told you about Tim. You were—bright and breezy.'

She managed to smile but twistedly. 'If you had any idea how exhausting it was, keeping myself bright and breezy…' She shook her head. 'I think that might have been another factor. I was mentally so tired.'

'Maisie—'

'No, please let me go on,' she begged. 'I could never find the words to explain to you—I didn't even know if it mattered to you—but Mairead was me responding to my music, the one area where I could shut everything else out…then I found in— in—' she rubbed her face '—in *dire* circumstances like Sonia's soirée, well, the only way I could cope was by extending that bubble a bit. I don't suppose I'm making any sense but—'

'You are,' he said very quietly. 'Can I tell you how it happened for me?'

'Yes, please,' she whispered.

'Everything that had ever plagued me disappeared when I saw you in that hospital bed. That's when I knew none of it carried any weight at all. That you were paramount to me and it was going to be sheer hell living without you.'

He raked a hand across his jaw. 'In fact, everything came together, Maisie, Mairead, they merged and became,' he paused, 'the only girl in the world for me. But that's when the agony really began.'

'Rafe?' She lifted her face to his and her eyes were green and incredulous. Her lips were trembling and she was shaking like a leaf in a gale. 'Tell me I'm not dreaming?'

He smiled fleetingly at last but he sobered immediately and touched her face with his fingertips. 'When I'm away from you I can't get you out of my mind, when I have you in my arms it couldn't feel more right. When I think of losing you, my whole world falls down and the only way to right it is to know that you belong to me and I belong to you.' He closed his eyes briefly. 'You could have no idea how ironic that is but it's true.'

'Tell me,' she whispered.

'I will one day but—'

'Excuse me.'

They both turned convulsively to see a man standing on the jetty, regarding them a trifle awkwardly.

He said, 'I heard the splashes and came running but you did the right thing climbing onto the boat. Then you seemed a little—um—preoccupied so I retreated but—uh—would this be your bag, though, miss? I found it on the jetty.'

'Oh, thank you!' Maisie breathed and Rafe reached over to take it. 'Thanks, mate,' he added.

'Are you both OK?'

'Fine, never better,' Rafe assured him. 'We actually make a habit of doing this.'

The stranger stared up at them then shrugged. 'If I were you I'd get dry and warm before you catch pneumonia.'

'Not a bad idea,' Rafe said gravely and turned to Maisie,

who was rather desperately trying not to laugh. 'You wouldn't have the keys for the boat in that bag by any chance, my love?'

'Y-yes,' she said a little unsteadily and pulled them from her bag.

They laughed together, standing in the middle of the *Amelie's* shipshape little saloon, standing in the circle of each other's arms, still dripping.

'He must think we're mad!' she said.

'He could be right. I'm certainly mad about you. I've done this once before without permission but I think it needs to be done again.' And he started to undress her.

She put her hand over his with a sudden cloud in her eyes. 'Susie…' And she told him what had happened to her phone. 'I should check in.'

'She's fine. I was talking to Grace only minutes before I bumped into you, just in case you'd checked in with her. Susie's had a bottle and she looks set to sleep for hours.'

Maisie relaxed. 'I love you too,' she told him and helped him out of his sodden jacket. 'We could have a shower— we should have a shower, and not only to continue a tradition we once established, and properly this time, but also to get warm and clean. See that little gas heater up on the wall there?'

He'd removed her sweater and he looked in the direction she was pointing. 'Uh-huh,' he said but distractedly because what he'd revealed was a pale lemon bra patterned with forget-me-nots.

'Well, it provides instant hot water.'

'Wonderful.' He turned his attention back to stripping her trousers off. 'Since,' he looked into her eyes, 'we've established that, may we proceed?'

'Please do,' she invited and a little glint lit her eyes. 'I was only keen to—set the scene.'

He paused and looked at her narrowly. 'You really want us to take a shower?'

'I really do. I had an amazing fantasy once about…showers—boat showers to be precise—so—'

He put his fingers to her lips. 'Say no more.' He ripped off the rest of his clothes, turned away to prime the gas heater then picked her up in his arms and carried her into the *Amelie's* bathroom.

It wasn't as large or as grand as the *Mary-Lue's* but the jet of water, after a few preliminary splutters, was warm and wonderful as it streamed over them.

Maisie took her bra off and her knickers and stood revelling in it. Then she looked into his eyes and saw a question in them. She turned the water off, wound her arms around him and pressed her breasts against the hard wall of his chest as she offered him her mouth.

The result was dynamite. Their kiss was everything she'd fantasised about. His hands on her sleek, slippery body were everything she'd dreamt about as tremors of desire rose from deep within her.

The hard months slipped away and she felt at last as if she'd reached a safe shore, a haven, but not only that, one shot with rapture and pure pleasure.

When he lifted his head at last it was to ask her if she still believed she was dreaming.

'No,' she gasped. 'Oh, no! But—would you mind not stopping? Because that was pure magic.'

He laughed softly. 'There's actually no stopping me now but we need a bed. Come.'

* * *

The double bunk on the *Amelie* was also in the aft berth and, again, not as luxurious as the *Mary-Lue's*, but perfectly adequate for two people who were setting each other alight.

'Do you have any express wishes in this instance?' he queried as he stroked her from head to toe and all the sensitive, wonderfully erotic places in between.

Maisie drew a shaky breath because Rafe was looking down at her with tenderness and laughter as if it was a private joke only they could share.

'I have had one overriding wish for a long time now.' She rubbed her cheek against his shoulder.

He put his fingers beneath her chin and tilted her face to his. 'Tell me.'

'Just to be openly in love with you and relaxed and happy about it.'

His eyes softened and he kissed her. 'Still?' he queried against the corner of her mouth.

'Mmm... Do you have any express wishes?'

'Yes. You've just put it into words.'

'Oh, Rafe.' She felt herself melt beneath her own rush of tenderness and she cupped the side of his face in her hand.

And that was the mood that claimed them as they kissed and made a timeless exploration of each other.

And although they could have been anywhere, Maisie began her own journey into a sea of delight.

He told her things she would never have guessed. Such as how he'd been almost unbearably tempted to make love to her after Sonia's soirée. Such as the iron discipline he'd had to exercise the night they'd slept in each other's arms at the muster camp.

'No,' she breathed.

'Yes,' he contradicted as he cupped her hips and cradled

her to him. And she looked into his eyes to see he was looking at her with heavy-lidded desire, and, just as she'd once antici-pated, it sent her to the moon…

And all the pent-up hunger she'd suffered, to have his hands on her, his body on hers, was released, making her move in his arms, making her offer her body to him with sheer pleasure and an urgent desire to please.

Until they were moving as one more and more urgently as their desire peaked and the sensations she'd never experi-enced before started to wash through her, filling her with the incredulous delight that she couldn't hide.

He saw it in her eyes just before they came together and he was moved beyond words as they shuddered simulta-neously in the ultimate release.

She was the first to break the rapturous silence.

'Rafe?' she whispered with her eyes closed. 'You were wonderful.'

He kissed her eyelids. 'We were, Maisie.' He touched ev-erything he loved about her—her red curls, her smooth skin now damp and dewy—and, with a little growl in his throat, he pulled her very close again.

'I should have known right from the start that this was the way it should be. You *always* felt as if as if you were made to be right here.'

Maisie breathed deeply as she felt his heart beating heavily again and could only believe every word he'd said.

'I'll never want to be anywhere else,' she murmured.

'I've had an idea.' He smoothed some wayward curls be-hind her ear. 'Let's get married again. We can call it a reaffir-mation.' He looked into her eyes. 'A good idea?'

She smiled then looked apprehensive. 'Aren't you supposed to be away for a month on business?'

'That was a business trip I didn't really need to make. It
was an excuse because I was going crazy trying to keep my
distance from you.'

She relaxed. 'It's a lovely idea.'

They smiled into each other's eyes then they clung together
as if they could never get enough of each other…

Two weeks later, together with Sonia and Liam and their
children, and, of course, Susie, as well as Grace and Jack
Huston, Maisie and Rafe reaffirmed their vows in Vava'u.

The day before they'd hired a boat and cruised to the spot,
in a sunlit calm sea, where Tim Dixon had died a hero, to
scatter his ashes.

And the two weeks leading up to it had been a revelation
for Maisie. The depth of Rafe's passion for her amazed and
delighted her and brought forth her own passion.

But it was just as much the little things that delighted her.
Their mental unity, the little things they laughed over. Susie's
sudden discovery that there was a man in her life—Rafe—
who always needed to be greeted with her most charming
smile, was one of them.

Being able to hold hands for no reason other than they
wanted to, waking up at night with his reassuring presence beside her, and knowing she was no longer alone…

It was a simple ceremony on the beach. Maisie wore a long
sleeveless sea-green dress that matched her eyes; Rafe wore
a black shirt and cream jeans.

Most of the staff of The Tongan, who were choir members

of the church on the hill behind the resort, sang a joyful hymn unaccompanied, their voices soaring skywards.

And as they faced each other, her hands clasped in his, Rafe and Maisie looked deep into each other's eyes and said these words to each other—

> '*The ocean brought me peace*
> *The wind gave me energy*
> *The sun warmed my spirit*
> *The flowers showed me life*
> *But you made me feel love*
> Ofa atu—*I love you*'

There was hardly a dry eye amongst the onlookers as they went into each other's arms.

THE ROYAL HOUSE OF NIROLI

*...International affairs, seduction
and passion guaranteed*

VOLUME FOUR

The Tycoon's Princess Bride
by Natasha Oakley

Isabella Fierezza has always wanted to make a difference to the lives of the people of Niroli and she's thrown herself into her career. She's about to close a deal that will ensure the future prosperity of the island. But there's just one problem…

Domenic Vincini: born on the neighbouring, *rival* island of Mont Avellana, and he's the man who can make or break the deal. But Domenic is a man with his own demons, who takes an instant dislike to the perfect Fierezza princess…

Worse, Isabella can't be in the same room with him – without wanting him! But if she gives in to temptation, she forfeits her chance of being queen…and will tie Niroli to its sworn enemy!

Available 5th October 2007

*...International affairs, seduction
and passion guaranteed*

VOLUME FIVE

Expecting His Royal Baby
by Susan Stephens

Nico Fierezza: as an internationally successful
magnate, he's never needed to rely on his family's
royal name. But now he's back – and the King has
matched him with a suitable bride. Niroli is ready
to welcome its new ruler!

Carrie Evans has been in love with Nico, her
boss, for years. But, after one magical night of loving,
he ruthlessly discarded her...and now she's
discovered she's carrying his child!

*Everything is in place for Nico's forthcoming nuptials.
But there's an unexpected wedding guest: Carrie, who is
willing to do anything to protect the future of her baby...
The question is – does anything include marrying Nico?*

Available 2nd November 2007

www.millsandboon.co.uk

M&B

4 FREE

BOOKS AND A SURPRISE GIFT!

We would like to take this opportunity to thank you for reading this Mills & Boon® book by offering you the chance to take FOUR more specially selected titles from the Modern™ series absolutely FREE! We're also making this offer to introduce you to the benefits of the Mills & Boon® Reader Service™—

- ★ FREE home delivery
- ★ FREE gifts and competitions
- ★ FREE monthly Newsletter
- ★ Exclusive Reader Service offers
- ★ Books available before they're in the shops

Accepting these FREE books and gift places you under no obligation to buy, you may cancel at any time, even after receiving your free shipment. Simply complete your details below and return the entire page to the address below. You don't even need a stamp!

YES! Please send me 4 free Modern books and a surprise gift. I understand that unless you hear from me, I will receive 6 superb new titles every month for just £2.89 each, postage and packing free. I am under no obligation to purchase any books and may cancel my subscription at any time. The free books and gift will be mine to keep in any case.

P7ZED

Ms/Mrs/Miss/Mr ....Initials ....

BLOCK CAPITALS PLEASE

Surname ....

Address ....

....

....Postcode..................................

Send this whole page to:
UK: FREEPOST CN81, Croydon, CR9 3WZ

Offer valid in UK only and is not available to current Mills & Boon® Reader Service™ subscribers to this series. Overseas and Eire please write for details and readers in Southern Africa write to Box 3010, Pinegowie, 2123 RSA. We reserve the right to refuse an application and applicants must be aged 18 years or over. Only one application per household. Terms and prices subject to change without notice. Offer expires 31st December 2007. As a result of this application, you may receive offers from Harlequin Mills & Boon and other carefully selected companies. If you would prefer not to share in this opportunity please write to The Data Manager, PO Box 676, Richmond, TW9 1WU.

Mills & Boon® is a registered trademark owned by Harlequin Mills & Boon Limited.
Modern™ is being used as a trademark. The Mills & Boon® Reader Service™ is being used as a trademark.